NEED ME

M. MALONE

CONTENTS

NEED ME

Happily-ever-afters aren't for the girl who has to measure her life between doctor's appointments. But don't cry for me, Argentina. I've made a game of seeing how far I can push before guys go running. Until I meet one who just keeps coming back.

He makes me laugh. He listens. And all the crazy stuff I do doesn't even faze him. Which is a problem when I find out he has the power to ruin my best friend's career. So I'm taking the gloves off. It's time for Operation: Get Rid of Mr. Perfect.

If being crazy didn't get rid of him maybe I have to try the scariest thing of all.

Being myself.

I

HOW IT STARTED

Ariana

COMFORTING YOUR BEST FRIEND DURING A BREAKUP is a time-honored tradition. Only it's never the way they portray it in the movies. There's no uplifting music playing in the background and we never conveniently have vodka and Chunky Monkey on hand.

Instead I'm sitting on the couch, trying to pretend my bestie doesn't have snot on her face. Meanwhile her tears are soaking through my shirt onto my bare skin.

It's about as non-cinematic as it gets.

The worst part? I'm still not exactly sure what happened.

"And *ohmygodyouwontbelieve*," Mya huffs between shaky breaths, her curly black hair flying around her face where it's come loose from her braid.

This has been the pattern ever since I got home from work to find her crying in her room. I've had this date on my calendar since last year. I figured she might need consolation on what *should* have been her wedding day. Her ex-boyfriend was a jerk who was terrible in bed. Or at least that was my assumption considering how little noise I heard when he slept over.

After she started seeing her new guy, I'd figured she was over it and wouldn't care when this day came. But I guess it finally caught up with her.

I nod along absently. "I'm so sorry. He was such a skeeze."

"No, I said you won't *believe* what he did." Mya pauses to blow her nose, honking loudly.

My dog, Oreo, skitters away at the loud sound. She curls up in the kitchen, looking like a black and white ball of fluff on top of her little dog bed.

"I can't believe Will would show his face on this day of all days. Wow, what a jerk."

"Will *was* here actually but that's not what happened. It's Milo. We were getting ready for our big presentation," she pauses to hiccup, "He stole the client. I can't believe I trusted him."

My mouth falls open. I have to admit that even I didn't see that one coming.

Mya and her boyfriend started out as office frenemies until the day she caught him at the company Happy Hour with his pants down. Literally.

When she came home and told me she'd seen what he was packing, I knew then what was coming. But she couldn't just have a little fun on the side. *Nooooo*, she had to go and fall in love with the guy. I was worried about her starting a new relationship but they *seemed* so solid.

Which just proves that I'm going soft.

"I'm sorry, sweetie. Maybe there's an explanation." It sounds weak even as I say it.

Mya sighs. "I know the explanation. He's an ass."

She grumbles as she gets off the couch and heads for the kitchen. At least she's not still under her blanket watching Netflix. It's not easy to know how to comfort someone when you have very little experience with what they're going through. I don't do relationships and have long held the belief that men are best seen (naked) and not heard.

Which doesn't explain the odd twist in the bottom of my gut. It's not that I'm jealous of Mya. Especially since she's currently eating cereal straight from the box with feral intensity. But I can't pretend there isn't a small part of me that wishes I felt as deeply about anything as she does about Milo.

"I have to run some errands."

Mya doesn't respond to my proclamation, which is just as well since it's complete bullshit. I just need to get out of this apartment. I walk back to my room where I quickly change clothes into a pair of tight black jeans and a black camisole. Just dressy enough for where I'm going but still comfortable.

There's this fancy hotel bar downtown where I like to hang out when I need to be alone. The bartenders at the Fitz-Harrington all know me and there aren't as many handsy guys to deter. The rich businessmen who hang out there are usually too worried about making a scene to do much when I shut them down. I should be able to drink alone in peace while I figure out how to purge these unwanted and unexpected longings for ... something.

My phone dings with a calendar reminder.

One Week: Doctor's appointment 10 a.m.

I swipe it away without even looking at it. As if I could forget. Ugh.

Mya barely looks up from her perch on the couch as I leave. The door closes behind me cutting off the sound of the sappy movie she's rewatching for the third time. Luckily I don't see anyone I know as I skip down the stairs and push open the front door of the building. I don't feel like talking.

I just want to walk and feel alive.

The night air is humid but it still feels good on my skin. July is not exactly picturesque weather in Washington DC since all the concrete makes the city feel like an oven on broil. But stepping out feels like freedom. People watching is one of my favorite pastimes.

After a short metro ride, I take the escalator up to street level. I can only hope my favorite bartender is working tonight. Frankie is this older, ex-Navy SEAL grump who always acts like his tuxedo is strangling him. I'm not sure how he got the job considering he's not very friendly and glares at all the customers but having him there quickly elevated the Fitz to one of my favorite places.

The bar is through the lobby and I smile politely at the hostess before pointing at the bar. She moves aside so I can enter. It's still relatively early so there are only a few people in the restaurant section and just one guy at the bar. He doesn't look up when I sit down.

"How's it going, Frankie?"

The bartender lifts his chin in greeting before preparing my usual order of a club soda with lime. I don't even have to say anything and I know he'll keep the drinks coming and the conversation to a minimum.

Like I said, one of my favorite places.

Sitting allows me to relax and think about all the changes coming in my life. I've been working mainly in the neonatal unit of the hospital for the past year now. Recently, I started thinking about making a change. After a lot of reflection, I decided to switch to working in the emergency room. Nursing is hard work, physically and emotionally. I was foolish to think that seeing so much devastation every day wouldn't eventually take its toll.

Not that emergency will be any easier but at least I'll be working with adults. There's something about watching babies suffer that has torn a chunk out of my spirit. For the first time ever, I thought about taking a break and living off the absolutely ridiculous trust fund my father made available to me when I turned eighteen.

But that felt too much like proving him right. So the money sits unused and I continue to make my own way.

Alone. Just the way I like it.

Bars get a bad rap. Most people think of dark, smelly, loud places with bad food and watered down liquor. But they're my favorite places to think. You can walk into a bar and sit alone and no one judges or asks any questions. Until you inevitably get one of those guys who can't take a hint.

"Hey baby. Is this seat taken?"

A man slides onto the stool next to me without waiting for my answer. He's got long, floppy brown hair and the glassy eyes of someone who is not quite drunk but getting there. He's wearing a suit like most of the men who hang out in this hotel but he still looks like he's only fifteen years old.

"Seriously, Frankie. Don't you guys card in here?"

He glances over at the guy before rolling his eyes. Which means he's definitely already checked the guy's ID. Otherwise, my college-aged neighbor would be outside on the sidewalk.

"Come on, don't be like that baby. I'm just trying to get to know you."

"I have a boyfriend."

"He's not here. If you were my girl, you'd never have to drink alone."

"Wow, you are really setting the bar high."

His brow wrinkles like he's trying to figure out if what I said is a good thing or a bad thing.

"You come here often?"

Oh geez, this guy isn't even trying. Usually I'll let them talk for a while before I send them packing but this guy doesn't even deserve a chance. I groan a little. Why are the most unimaginative guys always the most persistent?

"Every night. I've been waiting for you." I take the salt shaker and start pouring little lines in the shape of triangles on the bar in front of him.

"*Mmmm sola shaka ley. Mmmm sila shaka ley.*" I start whispering more nonsense words in the most ominous tone I can muster.

"Whoa lady, what the hell are you doing?" His eyes go to the shapes drawn on the bar. "Are you casting a spell?"

If his eyes get any wider they'll pop out of his head and roll onto the floor. He glances around frantically as if trying to see if anyone else notices what's happening.

That makes me want to laugh even more than his reaction. There's no one around to care and even if there was, rich people are great at ignoring anything that makes them uncomfortable. No one makes eye contact.

"Of course I'm casting a spell! How else can I make sure you never leave me?"

The guy immediately gets up and walks away. A snicker from my other side draws my attention. When I first sat down I barely noticed the guy other than his thick, dark hair. His head had been resting in his hand like he'd had a bad day.

Now he's sitting up straight and staring right at me.

The fact that he's so handsome shouldn't be as much of a surprise as it is. His dark hair has the perfect amount of curl and his eyes are a honey brown like good whiskey. It's the kind of male beauty that belongs on billboards and makes even smart women feel stupid.

"That was effective. I have to give you credit for that. The salt was a nice touch."

Frankie clearly doesn't agree as he appears with a wet rag and cleans up the salt. The guy slides a few bills across the bar, which softens Frankie's annoyance considerably.

"You didn't have to do that. I should have, since it was my mess. It just seemed easier than waiting for him to figure out it wasn't going to happen."

He shrugs. "It was entertaining. Better than the last movie I saw. Although that's probably not saying much since I get out less than my grandmother."

"Workaholic?" As soon as I ask, I wish I hadn't.

Asking a guy personal questions is like putting a green light on your forehead. But luckily the suit doesn't take it as a sign that I'm hot for him. He just sighs and looks down at his phone.

"Workaholic but I love it. I work for the family business so..." He shrugs again but something about the look in his eyes is familiar. It reminds me of what I've been feeling lately. Like I'm trapped and there's no way out.

"Family can be complicated." I think of my feuding parents, both too busy to care about me unless of course they think it'll hurt the other in some way.

"I'm not complaining." He shakes his head. "At least I get to do something I'm good at every day. It would just be nice... never mind."

"No, what? You can tell me." I'm not sure why I care but suddenly all I want is for him to finish that sentence. For someone else to put a name to this restless feeling.

"It would be nice to feel more fulfilled. Like what I'm doing actually matters to someone." He closes his eyes briefly, like he didn't mean to reveal so much.

"Yes. I get that."

He opens his eyes. "This is quite heavy for bar talk."

I laugh at that. "True. Should I ask if you come here often instead?"

"That was particularly uninspiring, I have to agree. Is that usually how men hit on you?"

"Most of them try a little harder than that. But salt always does the trick."

He covers his mouth with his hand. "I noticed. You like to cause a bit of trouble, *bella*? Beautiful little devil."

"Italian. I wondered where your accent was from."

He looks alarmed. "Is it noticeable?"

"No. Your English is amazing. I can just hear a little something on certain words."

He relaxes at that. "I've worked hard to lose it. It's helpful in business to speak English like you've been to boarding school."

"That's very specific."

"Tell me about it. The rules never end it seems. I'm Vin."

"Like Vincent?"

"No."

His refusal to give me anything else peaks my interest. This guy has game. He knows how to give just enough to gain my attention without making me feel like he's the type to get overly attached and want me to meet his mother after the first date.

Then again, with a face like his, he's probably the one running away from stage-five clingers.

"I'm Ariana."

I brace myself for more questions. Usually I don't want to encourage that much interest but this time maybe I'll actually answer them.

He hums. "You like to push people away. Men like that make it easy I imagine."

Stunned and feeling a little vulnerable at his spot on assessment, I turn the statement back around.

"I'm not pushing people away. I'm simply not going to waste my time on someone I'm not attracted to."

He looks shocked. "Wow. So if he'd been attractive you wouldn't have put a spell on his ancestors?"

It's a struggle not to smile. But I refuse to give him any points when he's trying to make me feel bad for the same thing men do all the time. People love to make women feel that coddling men's feelings is their responsibility. But you won't see men doing the same for us and they'll never feel guilty about that.

"Men don't hit on women if they aren't physically attracted. They go for what they want, when they want. All I'm doing is the exact same thing."

"This is true. So you like to get straight to it, huh?"

If he's expecting me to be ashamed, he came to the wrong bar. Owning my sexuality is probably the only positive thing my mother ever taught me. I'll never allow a man to make me feel ashamed of the same needs they flaunt with no repercussions.

"Men can't be trusted to stick around so what's the point? I might as well get the one thing I actually need and then go home."

There's something in his eyes I can't pinpoint. It almost looks like disappointment. Maybe he's just not used to people telling it like it is.

"Maybe one day a man will surprise you."

He only reminds me of what I can't have. Plans. A future. All the things I learned not to hope for.

All at once I am tired. People who have a good support system have no idea how exhausting it is to be on your own. Every decision, every mistake and even every triumph is a weight you carry on your back. Sometimes I wish I could drop everything and run away screaming at the top of my lungs. But since I can't do that, I settle for living in the moment.

"Do you want to get out of here?"

I've surprised him. He stares like he's trying to see if I'm really on board with going home with a stranger. But this is how I have to live my life. In the moment.

Right now.

So if this is all I can have, then I want it all.

2

Din

DISCREETLY, I BREATHE INTO MY HAND. MEETING someone, especially someone like her, was the last thing I expected when I came out tonight. I'd just needed some fresh air away from my hotel room and all the work I hadn't finished.

But now here I am, alone with a captivating, slightly insane woman and I desperately need a toothbrush.

"So, uh, I'll be right out. Just going to use the restroom."

We're in one of the Fitz's standard rooms. Ariana suggested we get a room at the hotel and I definitely wasn't going to bring her up to the penthouse suite I usually shared with my brother when we were in town. Clearly she wasn't kidding when she said she liked to get right to the point.

She also had a system. The bartender had thoroughly reviewed my identification before nodding at her. His approval apparently meant something. Or he was her safety contact if anything should happen to her. Both I could understand. The guy had glared at me so long I felt my life flash before my eyes.

"Maybe I'll sage the room while you're gone. You know, get rid of any bad vibes."

I can't help but return her grin. She's enjoying this and so am I, although I'll be damned if I know why.

Once I'm safely behind the closed bathroom door, I rub my sweaty palms together. In an expensive hotel like this there should be complimentary toiletries, even in the basic rooms. I see the usual array of soaps and hair products on the counter next to a stack of towels.

No toothbrush.

When I bend down to look under the vanity there's nothing but toilet paper. And only a paltry two extra rolls at that.

I suppose budget cuts have affected all businesses in this economy.

This woman is every man's fantasy. Like a walking wet dream and completely opposed to seeing me after today. When I asked her for her number, she just raised a perfectly sculpted eyebrow and shook her head.

On her, even rejection is sexy.

And I'm going to have to go back out there with stale breath and a churning stomach.

This is not the time to screw things up. I have to get it together. So why the hell am I so wound up? Being with her feels different somehow and it's throwing me off my game in a major way.

Working for my famous older brother has its perks. The name Philippe might not ring any bells but due to Andre's success in the fashion world our last name, Lavin, has become synonymous with style. I get to travel the globe representing our company and convincing buyers across continents they need to carry our clothes.

We live life in the fast lane and I've always loved it.

Until lately.

There is a time to overthink things and a time for action. I can analyze the details later. Right now, I need to go peel the clothes off the perfect little treat waiting in the bed and show her why Italian men have an international reputation for being excellent lovers.

When I come out of the bathroom, I pause in the doorway.

My fiery little devil is curled up on the bed sleeping.

I pull the covers over her gently. Spying a notepad next to the bed, I quickly write a note before I change my mind.

You needed sleep more than anything I could give you.

I scribbled my phone number underneath.

As I close the door to the hotel room behind me, I am a mass of confusion. I just left a beautiful troublemaker to sleep alone.

What the hell is wrong with me?

But there had been something in her eyes when she'd declared that all men were a disappointment. Maybe it made me a fool but I wanted to be the man who surprised her.

Or at least not the man who proved her theory right once again.

As I ride the elevator up to the penthouse level, I have a feeling my decision to ignore my hormones will haunt me for the rest of the night. But giving my right hand a workout won't be so bad with an image of Ariana sleeping soft and rumpled in my head.

Being so aroused by everything she does should be alarming but truthfully I'm more worried that I'd really wanted to climb in with her and hold her until morning.

From the outside looking in, my life seems like a movie. Money, cars, girls and good times. Everyone wants a piece of the Lavin pie and they'll do anything to get it.

When we first started it seemed like a long shot but my brother's design skill and my powers of persuasion proved to be an invincible combination. Our achievements have gone beyond our wildest dreams.

But we didn't know then how it would change our lives, the good and the bad. The people who only want you for what you can offer. The friends who fall away and the ones who reappear when it's convenient.

It's been a long time since I met someone who wasn't interested in what my last name could provide.

Despite every inch of me clamoring to go back and wake her up, I have the feeling this won't be the last time I see my little temptress. I believe in destiny and something tells me I won't have to wait long before she calls me.

Whatever this is between us is too good to ignore.

The next morning is busy and I spend an hour on the phone with a buyer in London. Fashion never sleeps and a company like my brother's is no exception. Andre has been making clothes since he was a teenager, even though everyone around him found it strange that he would bother.

Our mother had a team of stylists and tailors to outfit the family for the many social events we were required to attend each season. If she only knew how much we hated those events. Then again, my mother isn't known for being sensitive to our needs. She loves us and she loved our father deeply until the day he died, but Sofia Lavin is a demanding woman.

Demanding women seem to be my type. I imagine my beautiful little troublemaker from the bar waking up to find me gone. She's managed to sneak into my thoughts more than a few times since last night. Not just because she was stunning. Beautiful women are part of life in the fashion world.

No, there was something more about her, something inde-finable that made her shine brighter than anyone else.

Maybe the only reason I wanted her number was because I'm not used to being told no. But it's also because she was just so... unexpectedly delightful. I had fun talking to her, something that hasn't happened in quite some time.

Most of the women I meet are more interested in impressing me, showing off how long their legs are and in securing an invitation to meet my brother.

Always my brother. His celebrity eclipses everything in his orbit, including me.

But this time, Andre wasn't even part of the equation because she didn't know who I was. Remembering her with that salt shaker makes me chuckle. Definitely didn't know who I was. None of the models in our social circle would cast spells as a means to deter unwanted male attention. To most models attention is a currency they can never collect enough of.

I still can't believe I told a stranger I felt unfulfilled.

My phone shows no missed calls or messages when I check. I was expecting to get a text when she woke up. Is it possible that she didn't see my note?

"Philippe? Are you ready?" Andre leans his head in and then nods when I stand.

Meetings and more meetings are all I have to look forward to today.

But hopefully before it's all over, I'll have a date.

3

Ariana

Opening my eyes in an unfamiliar place is on my list of things I'd rather not do. So when I wake up, it's like a gunshot went off. I jackknife straight up in bed, looking around frantically.

Horrified, I swipe a bit of drool off my cheek. What the hell is going on? How long have I been asleep?

But no answers are forthcoming because I can tell instantly that no one else is in the room.

The covers are tucked around me, a fact I only discover when they twist around my legs as I stand. Still a bit disoriented, I glance around the room. It's a pretty standard hotel room with a bed, a desk against the opposite wall and a television.

As usual, the bedside table has a phone and a notepad with the hotel's logo at the top. I squint to see the message written there.

"Dude, your handwriting looks like a serial killer. Or maybe a doctor."

Some of the doctors I've worked with over the years had handwriting you'd need a decoder ring to figure out. After peering at it for a while I manage to figure out what it says.

You needed sleep more than anything I could give you.

He'd written his phone number below the message. Clearly he hadn't believed me when I said I didn't want to exchange numbers. Not that I can blame him. I wouldn't have believed me either. The man looks like an underwear model and I haven't even seen him without his clothes. A naked Vin is probably even more spectacular.

"He tucked me in. Who does that?" Instead of hot sex, he'd put me to bed and left. I'm not sure if that makes him even weirder than I am or just... a nice person.

The thought of never seeing him naked makes me depressed but I keep a no numbers policy for a reason. There are no relationship expectations and no chances for anyone to get attached or get their feelings hurt. I crumple the note in my fist and throw it away before I'm tempted to take it with me.

I have the policy for a very good reason but this is the first time I've ever actually regretted it.

Luckily an Uber is close by so I don't have to linger long waiting for a ride. When I get home, the apartment is quiet. Mya isn't awake yet so at least I don't have to answer any questions about how my night went.

Usually I'm happy to scandalize my slightly uptight bestie with tales of my hot one night stands but this time I feel strangely protective over the details.

Which doesn't make any sense.

This is exactly the kind of weird story I'd usually love to share.

But the way Vin stared into my eyes while we were talking doesn't seem like the kind of thing you share over girl talk for a laugh.

"There you are!" Mya suddenly appears in the kitchen. She glances at me and then at the front door. "Did you just get in?"

"I needed to go to the store." I escape before she has time to look in the fridge and see that it's still pretty empty.

That night, I have the place all to myself again because Mya got a message from her client that he wanted to meet for dinner. I'm thrilled her situation seems to be working itself out.

Since the client called her, maybe the whole thing was a misunderstanding. I hope so. Even though relationships aren't my thing, watching her mope on the couch made me regret not being more supportive. Mya has never been as happy as she is with Milo and so I told her to give the guy a chance to explain.

Anything is better than watching my best friend's heart break a little more each day.

Besides, someone needs to get the happily-ever-after around here. How else am I going to be the cool Aunt to her sure-to-be-adorable future kids?

I check my phone and see a bunch of voicemails. My parents are the only ones who insist on calling instead of texting like everyone else. It wouldn't be so bad if they were checking on me or asking about how my life is going. Instead it's always long, rambling messages about how much they hate each other.

Even before their divorce, my father traveled so much that I didn't see him often. My mother on the other hand was way too present in my life, one of the reasons I applied to colleges across the country. I got lucky when I found this apartment and the neighborhood, Adams Morgan, is a fun place with lots of cool restaurants and nightlife.

Its best feature is being a five-hour flight from Beverly Hills.

Well, if I have to listen to their bitching, it might as well be amusing.

My father, originally from Venezuela, is the proverbial workaholic business mogul who had no idea how to relate to a little girl. He usually just asks if I need more money. He thinks everything can be solved with a check.

I go into my contacts and change *Eduardo Silva* to *Daddy Warbucks*.

My mother, originally from Sweden, is a former model whose only hobby is complaining about my father's new wife. Or in her words, *the hussy who fucked my husband in our vacation house.* She manages to turn every single thing into a huge deal and of course expects me to be on her side every time. She's what Mya would call a Drama Llama.

Smiling, I change *Ingrid Larsson* to *Drama Mama*.

I push the button to play the messages while the water warms up for my shower.

Daddy Warbucks: Your mother keeps calling in the middle of the night. It's upsetting Veronica. If she needs more money tell her–

MESSAGE DELETED

Drama Mama: Your father's home-wrecking hussy wants you to take pictures with them. As if you're her daughter. The nerve! The absolute nerve–

MESSAGE DELETED

Daddy Warbucks: I forgot to tell you Veronica would like for you to take some pictures with us. Our therapist says we need to bond as a family–

MESSAGE DELETED

After a shower and a pep talk, I've changed into a clean set of scrubs for my first day working in the Emergency Room. I take a deep breath and regard myself with critical eyes in the bathroom mirror.

Change is here and I'm ready for it.

For years I've heard from nurse friends that the pace of emergency is different. Not that it wasn't busy in the NICU but this is on a totally different level.

In just the first hour of my shift we had two gunshot wounds, a heart attack and a suspected domestic assault. Things slowed a little giving me hope and then started all over again when there was a wave of injuries from a bar brawl. One of the guys had a piece of glass stuck in his face so close to his eye that it was a miracle he could see.

Why did I think this would be less heartbreaking?

"You've had a rough first day, kid. And I was hoping to convince you to leave that agency and go full-time here." Jackie, the nurse supervisor, pauses to enter something in the computer.

"This is definitely something."

"I know you're about to leave but can you take this one first? Suspected wrist fracture and possible concussion. They gave him something for pain in the ambulance." She hands me the next chart. "Guy got hit by a car."

"Sure thing." When I see the name on the chart I chuckle. The patient's name is listed as Mickey Mouse.

Jackie smiles, too. "You noticed. We have a comedian. Or a criminal. But I hope it's the first."

I'm so busy looking over the patient's chart that I don't notice anything odd at first. Then I look up and gasp.

"You!"

Vin grins deliriously. "I knew it. I am in heaven. Or maybe hell if my little devil is here."

I glance behind me to make sure Jackie isn't close by. The last thing I need on my first day in a new department is to be the subject of gossip.

"What are you doing here? Did you follow me or something?"

He holds up his arm and I gasp at the sight of the bloody, ripped fabric wrapped around his forearm.

"Oh my god. You're actually hurt." Instantly I feel like the worst kind of bitch.

"I seem to be bleeding," he mumbles, before squinting down at his arm like he's not sure why it looks that way.

"Okay, let's get you checked in so the doctor can take a look at this arm."

He startles a little when I come closer with the blood pressure cuff. "It was me vs. taxicab. The cab won this time."

"I see that. Any reason you were walking in traffic?"

He snorts. "I was trying to hail a ride and didn't see this guy pulling up so fast. That'll teach me to look where I'm going and stop daydreaming about blondes with smart mouths."

I'm not touching that comment so I focus on taking his vitals.

"But it brought me here so that means I was right."

"About what?"

He points at me with his good hand. "This. Us. I was just thinking about you and now you're here. It must be fate."

Although he's really cute when he's delirious, what he says just proves I was right not to keep his number.

He's a keeper. The kind of guy who says he can do casual but always ends up getting serious. Before you know it he's buying a ring and bringing you home to mama.

And I am not the kind of girl you bring home.

It bums me out though because he's gorgeous and fun. I take a moment to mourn the night of nakedness we never got to have. But I have to do the right thing and let him go. He believes in good winning over evil and the universe putting people together.

He deserves someone with that same optimism not a girl who believes that life likes to kick us while we're down.

"Why did you put a fake name? Are you in some kind of trouble?"

He shrugs. "I like cartoons. Is my brother here? My brother should be here soon."

That's my cue to leave. Letting him go means meeting the family is definitely not on my to-do list tonight or ever.

"Vin?"

"Hmm?" His eyes are still slightly unfocused and there's a fine sheen of sweat on his forehead.

I'm glad he has someone coming to get him because I would really feel bad about sneaking off if he was all alone.

That's a feeling I know all too well and I wouldn't wish it on anyone.

"Take care of yourself, okay? Be happy and don't walk in front of any more cabs."

"No traffic. Got it."

He looks so lost and rumpled sitting there that it's hard to resist giving him a final hug. But instead I just pat his shoulder gently.

"Bye."

Jackie looks up when I come back out. My expression must be giving away more than I realized because she stops typing.

"Is everything okay? Mickey isn't giving you any trouble is he?"

I take a deep breath and then shake my head. "This is kind of embarrassing but that guy is ... we went on a date recently and it didn't end well. I just needed to get out of there."

She hums in understanding. "Honey, we've all been there. Go on and clock out. I'll take care of him."

Ten minutes later, I come back from the locker room changed into street clothes. Jackie is talking to a tall, dark-haired man. That must be Vin's brother, which means he'll be discharged soon.

I turn and walk the other way.

It was a total fluke that I happened to be on shift when he got hurt but working in the hospital, you see people you know more often than you'd think.

It's tempting to hang around for one final glimpse of him. The thought that I'll never see him again hangs over me like a cloud.

But this is the way things have to be.

4

Din

THERE'S THUNDER IN MY HEAD.

And a lightning bolt in my arm.

Only no one notices my torment. I watch through hazy eyes as they all smile at my brother. Andre peers down at me with concern, his eyes taking in the splint on my wrist before running over my face. Once he's satisfied I'm in no immediate danger, he spares a smile for the women hovering at his elbow.

"Thank you for calling me, ladies. I was most distressed to hear there was an accident. I'm still not sure why he told you his name was ... what was it?"

"Mickey Mouse!" The bubbly redheaded nurse flinches when the older woman going over my chart glares at her.

"Back to work everyone!"

They all scramble to leave but not before one of the women touches Andre's sleeve and then squeals with excitement. He clears his throat before carefully extricating his arm. It's a curious thing but I've observed it many times before. People feel compelled to touch him almost like they can't believe he's real unless they do.

"Mr. Lavin, now that I'm aware of who you are, I can understand why your brother put down a false name."

Andre puts a comforting hand on my shoulder. "Yes, I'm sure he was just trying to prevent any commotion in your hospital. Perhaps there is a way we can leave without attracting too much attention."

"I'll see what I can do." The older woman's attention swings to me then. "You're all set, hon. The doctor said you don't have a concussion so we're going to discharge you. Just make sure you take it easy. You got really banged up. Luckily your wrist wasn't broken."

I start laughing and then once I start, I can't stop. My body is bruised all the way down my left side, I have a sprained wrist and my head is splitting. Nothing about this day feels lucky.

It feels more like the universe tried to take me out and just happened to miss.

Thinking of that makes me wonder. If today had been my last day, what would I regret? The fog in my brain clears long enough for me to realize Ariana never came back.

"*Bella*, where are you? She has escaped once more."

Andre leans down to hear me. "What? Who escaped? Dear brother I think you might be high from the pain medication."

"Yeah, probably."

Accepting his arm, I stand carefully. The room spins and for a moment I'm convinced that everything I ate earlier is about to make an unwelcome appearance. But then the world turns right side up again and I take a deep breath. The air seems too thick, like I can barely take it in.

Hopefully I'll feel better once I'm away from this place and no longer have the smell of antiseptic and sadness in my nose.

This is not what I imagined my life would be as a young boy. Feeling trapped and restless in my work and even worse, jealous of my own brother. This is not what my father would have wanted for me. Thinking that he would be disappointed in the man I have become is unbearable.

"Do you believe in fate, Andre? Like the stories *Papa* used to tell?"

He sighs. "Tonight, I took a woman on a date. It was crashed by the man she was meant to be with. I believe fate drives us all where it wants us to go. It's just not always a pleasant ride."

It's not often my brother doesn't get the girl so this news is a surprise. It's petty but it actually makes me feel a little better.

"That means I'll see her again."

"What?"

I ignore his questioning glance. No one needs to know about my beautiful little devil. She's mine.

Spending days in bed is one of those things that's better in theory than reality. Honestly, it's my worst nightmare. My brother is very talented but a nursemaid he is not.

Thinking of nurses reminds me of Ariana. It was quite a shock to see her wearing scrubs but the best kind. I imagine there have been plenty of men who would walk in front of a cab on purpose if it meant being taken care of by a woman like her.

When she'd appeared in the midst of my pain and confusion, it had seemed like fate intervening once again. But then she'd slipped away and I still have no way to contact her outside of stalking the hospital hoping to see her. If this is fate's idea of pushing us together it's doing a terrible job.

I'll end up in a ditch instead of in her bed at this rate.

There's a quick knock at the door and I groan. Andre must have put in some kind of standing order with room service because they've been delivering a steady stream of boring food for each meal.

It's a struggle to stand after lazing around all day so it takes me a minute to get up. The man at the door makes quick work of wheeling the tray in and setting up the table. After signing the receipt, and including a healthy tip, I'm alone again.

I scowl down at the bowl of soup and the sleeve of crackers on the tray. If I never have to look at another bowl of soup or porridge again I'll be content.

Getting hit by a car was no picnic but I'm not dying. This food is making me feel like I have one foot in the grave already.

That's it. I'm going out. They told me that I should take it easy for a few days. They didn't say anything about treating me like a grandfather or boring me to death.

"Where are you going? You're supposed to be resting," Andre asks in Italian, gesturing to the bed.

We usually speak Italian when we're alone since he's not concerned about practicing his English. The Italian accent simply adds to his mystique and of course, women love it. Funny how the same people who admire the accent in social situations assume it means you're less competent in business negotiations.

I sigh. "I'm just going for a walk. I need to stretch my legs."

"I'll come with you."

"No!"

He looks a little hurt so I run a hand through my hair. It's not my brother's fault that his presence inevitably draws a crowd. But I can't deal with that today.

"You have a lot to do getting ready for the marketing launch. You don't need to babysit me. I'm just going to stretch my legs. Maybe find us some snacks. I'm sure there must be a shop or grocery close by."

He looks dubious at the idea. Probably just the idea of buying your own groceries is what's throwing him off. We are definitely spoiled by the lifestyle we grew up living.

"Okay, just be careful. Do you have your phone?"

"Yes, *Mamma*. Don't worry so. I'm a big boy now."

He scowls. "I would have thought so but then you walked in front of a taxi."

"Sorry about that. Especially since I pulled you away from the beautiful Mya."

"That wasn't going to happen anyway. But going to the agency for marketing meetings should be interesting going forward."

45

"You just had to hit on a woman working on the most important launch of our company's history?"

He's already walking away but he gives me the finger over his shoulder. I'm still chuckling by the time I change into a pair of jeans and a cashmere sweater from last year's line. It fits perfectly and is long enough to cover the bandages on my sprained wrist. I need to get out of here before Andre notices I'm wearing something that's out of season.

Once I'm out of the hotel, I use my phone to search out the closest grocery. Then I use the navigation to point me toward a place called Trader Joe's. Whenever we plan to spend extended time in a city, I always investigate the best clubs and restaurants but I've never really thought about things like groceries before. Living out of a hotel means you don't have to.

But today, I want to feel normal. I need to be around people and noise and life. As I walk, the chatter of the people I pass flows around me. The many different American accents are a fascinating jumble and then there are the occasional foreign accents thrown in. Being the capital, DC always maintains a healthy community of dignitaries and visitors from other countries along with many foreign exchange students. Although I know it's not Andre's favorite place, I always love it when we come here.

The entrance to the store is covered in a riot of flowers. The blooms are festive and my mood lifts instantly. Shoppers mill around outside looking at the potted plants and there are even bales of hay strewn around the displays. Before I came to America for the first time I'd imagined meeting cowboys on every corner. The reality wasn't quite as fun but I can admit to still carrying a bit of fascination for the idea even now.

Following the crowd, I take a little basket just like the woman in front of me. It shouldn't be that difficult to blend in. I'll just watch what everyone else does and then follow suit. There are large displays of vegetables set around the open space. It reminds me of the outdoor markets in Europe. The woman I'm following picks up some kind of melon and taps it.

Is that how you're supposed to choose fruit? I pick up a clump of bananas and tap them before placing them in my basket. This grocery thing isn't so bad. Next I see a display of large tomatoes. I tap several before choosing one that looks the biggest. A man in the aisle next to me stares as I pick up an orange and tap it.

Am I doing it wrong?

When I turn to observe how everyone else is picking fruits, I bump into the person behind me.

"Sorry, sir. I didn't see you."

The sweet voice doesn't match the devilish face that comes into view when I turn.

"Oh my god. You have got to be kidding me." Ariana waves the cucumber in her hand at me. "How does this keep happening?"

"I told you already. Fate."

5

Ariana

WHAT IS IT WITH THIS GUY? FIRST IN THE BAR, THEN in the hospital and now I can't even manhandle phallic-shaped veggies without him hanging over my shoulder.

He calls it fate. But it's probably more like karma. The universe seems to be having a good laugh shoving the one guy I might actually want in my face at the exact time in my life that I can't keep him.

That thought reminds me of the appointment I have coming up that I've been ignoring. With a sigh, I place the cucumber I've been waving around in my basket before moving on to the peppers.

"I hope you're making something that tastes better than the bland shit I've been eating lately."

He peers into my basket curiously before I can switch it to the other arm. His wrist still has a splint on it but his long sleeves cover most of it. He looks a little odd wearing a cashmere sweater when it's so hot outside and his hair definitely hasn't seen a brush in days but otherwise he looks like a slightly rumpled guy with a perfectly stubbled jaw.

I blow out a breath. The man really is too sexy for his own good. Which means I need to get rid of him. Stat.

"Is this a good orange?" He holds it up and taps the side, putting his ear next to the peel.

"What are you doing?"

"Tapping it. Isn't that how you do it? I saw a woman tapping her fruit so I thought it was supposed to sound a certain way."

Holding back a smile, I take the orange from his hand and place it in his basket. "You only tap certain fruits. Usually melons."

He looks disappointed. "Oh. And I was enjoying it so much."

As I move to the salad section, I'm acutely aware of him following closely. This can't really be a coincidence, can it? Seeing him in this many places in DC has to violate all the laws of probability. But I can't deny the little flash of pleasure that zipped through me when I saw him. He has a way of grinning that makes me feel it all the way down to my toes. Like seeing me has made his day.

It's the kind of thing that's really hard to forget.

When he reaches in the next display case for a single serving of salad, his sleeve moves back revealing the splint. I tell myself that I'm just checking him out in a medical sense, making sure he's really okay after his accident. When he catches me watching him, his lips curl.

"Keeping a close eye on me, *bella*?"

"I'm just looking at your wrist. You seem to be healing nicely. That's good."

His brow furrows. "That's it? You aren't going to ask how I felt about you abandoning me at the hospital?"

"I didn't abandon you. My shift was over and I had to go."

"Uh huh. Well, I was very hurt. First you fall asleep on me. Then you abandon me."

"I didn't–"

He continues, clearly on a roll now that I can't escape. "Your continued indifference to my feelings is very hard on me. Almost as hard as wanking with a sprained wrist. That was a real challenge. Thank you for asking."

"I wasn't going to ask. I figured you'd manage somehow."

He shrugs. "Being ambidextrous had to come in handy at some point."

Not wanting him to see my smile, I move away from the produce and suddenly notice all the people who *definitely* just heard what he said.

An older lady with her almost white hair styled in a profusion of rigid curls watches us with an open mouth. My face heats.

For the first time in years, I'm feeling something. It's unfamiliar but I think it might be… embarrassment?

He's done the impossible. He's managed to out-crazy me.

When Vin notices the older woman staring, he winks lazily. "*Buonasera*. I enjoyed watching you picking the fruit. I'm learning so much today."

She puts a hand to her mouth, clearly charmed. "Oh, stop."

I walk away quickly heading for the meat department. I'm debating whether I should just shove my head underneath all the packages of ground beef when Vin appears at my elbow.

"I would say I can't believe you just did that but... this is you. So yeah that just happened."

He follows as I grab what I need before moving on to get the cheese slices Mya likes so much. As soon as I pick them up I remember. She's back with Milo. That means I won't see her around much anymore. I put the cheese slices back with a sigh.

Vin grabs a bag of chips from a standing display. He puts them in his basket at an awkward angle, trying not to tip it over.

"I have to get snacks. Otherwise I'm eating nothing but the boring healthy shit my brother likes."

This is how easy it is to get taken in. Because I was about to ask him about his brother and what kind of foods they've been eating. Luckily I catch myself. Just because this guy is clearly a stalker doesn't mean that I have to play along.

We go through the self-checkout, with Vin drawing all the female clerks to "help" when he can't get his chips to scan properly. While they're busy, I bag my groceries at light speed and rush out.

I'm halfway across the parking lot when he appears behind me, breathing heavily.

"Wait! Just hold on."

When he bends over and looks pained, I instantly feel guilty. He got hit by a freaking car less than a week ago and now he's running after me in a parking lot.

"You shouldn't be running. Actually you shouldn't be out grocery shopping either. You're supposed to be resting and icing your wrist."

He straightens and starts walking next to me. "I'm tired of that. Besides, clearly I'm exactly where I'm supposed to be."

Not this again.

Maybe he's just not good at leaving things open-ended. Clearly he's a person who needs closure.

I stop and hold out my hand.

He blinks. "What is that?"

It takes actual effort to hold back an eye-roll.

"It's a handshake. Customary when saying goodbye to a virtual stranger."

"I'm not a stranger."

Instantly that look is back in his eye, the one that promises he's not going to back down. The fact that it makes me so happy is exactly why this needs to end now.

"You are. You're supposed to be. One night stands are supposed to be people you don't see again."

"We didn't have a one night stand."

"It was one night."

"Nothing happened other than me watching you sleep. Technically it was a zero night stand. That doesn't count."

Since I can't refute his logic, I focus on the real point. He wants the night we should have had. Is there really any point in pretending I don't want the same thing?

"A do-over might be possible."

We've reached my car and I hit the button to open the trunk. After loading all the bags, I turn to look at him. He's got that knowing look on his face like my nonchalant act isn't fooling him one bit.

Any man this hot knows what he's working with. I'm sure he's used to women throwing themselves at him all the time but if that's what he's waiting for he'll be standing here a long time.

"We can go back to the bar. Pretend we're meeting for the first time again."

He shakes his head immediately. "No bar. A real restaurant. I want to be able to hear you."

"Why? We both know what you really want. We might as well just pick a hotel."

"You seem like the kind of woman who can appreciate honesty. So I'm just going to put it out there. I don't want to take you to a hotel. I want to take you on a real date."

Stunned, I can't look away. There's an intensity in his eyes that demands I listen. I'm not sure anyone could walk away when a man like this is being so bravely vulnerable.

"Why? I mean you don't even know me," I say finally.

"I know. But I want to. Every time I see you, I feel things I've never felt. This is going to sound crazy but I believe in fate. To meet at the bar and then see you at the hospital and then *again* today. I don't think it's coincidence."

My heart speeds up at the same time as it sinks. Despite being outside, I suddenly feel like I can't get enough air. My face feels like it's on fire when he moves closer and takes my hand. His eyes are too intense and in them I see all the expectations and dreams that are more dangerous to me than any drug. It would be so easy to get wrapped up in the fantasy and let myself hope that for once, everything will work out perfectly.

Why did he have to appear in my life now? It hurts more to find someone amazing when you already know it can't last.

"This is too much. I can see in your eyes that it's too much. But all I'm asking for is a chance to spend more time with the girl I met in that bar. She was real. She was funny. And talking to her was the most fun I've ever had."

"Okay but I get to pick the restaurant."

The words come out before I even realize what I'm going to say. He squeezes my hand like he knows what I'm thinking.

"That's fine. I'm sure you know this city better than I do."

The triumphant look on his face says he thinks he's gotten one up on me. That he's finally scored a point. Which only proves how little he really knows. Because the more he makes me want him, the more determined I am to show him it's a bad idea.

"Meet me at Wilbur's tonight at eight o'clock."

"Fantastic. How should I dress? Suit? Jeans?"

This is almost too easy. "A suit for sure. It's the hottest reservation in the city. I know the owner so I can get us in."

He looks impressed. "Great. I'll see you there."

"I can't wait."

⁊⯎

That night I don't bother putting on makeup or a cute outfit. Vin wants the real me so he's going to get the real me. The night we met I was a little depressed and all out of fucks. What he got that night was the unrefined, uncut version of Ariana that usually works to keep people away.

Didn't work on him though, did it?

No, nothing about my mystery man from the bar has been the usual.

My phone dings with another calendar appointment.

Tomorrow: Doctor's appointment 10 a.m.

Location: Northern Virginia Oncology Partners

With a groan, I swipe it away so it disappears from the screen. The reminders are necessary but they are a serious buzzkill.

God, I'm not in the mood for this date. Especially since I know it's not going to end in the hot sex that would at least make me feel better before being poked and prodded tomorrow.

I feel a momentary pang that Vin couldn't just be like all the rest. If he'd been happy with one night, at least I would get to have the memory of being with him to keep me warm on future cold nights.

But he had to give that absolutely dreamy speech earlier about fate and wanting the real me. Well, it's doubtful he'll feel that way after tonight.

Wilbur's is this awesome barbecue place that has a huge pig on the sign outside. The guy probably wears silk boxers to bed. I doubt he's ready to chow down on barbecue and get sauce all over his face.

It's almost time to leave. I open my closet and pull out the finishing touch for my outfit. Wait until he gets his first look at just how crazy I can get. Imagining Vin's reaction is totally worth going on this date.

Washington DC is similar to most big cities in that space is at a premium. Women traveling alone are at particular risk for guys who use it as an excuse to get too close.

After one too many *accidental* ass-grabs on the metro, I devised a system to gain myself some space. It's amazing how hard people will work to stay away if you seem strange enough. My little accessory keeps anyone from getting too close. But tonight it has a different purpose.

This is the final nail in the scare-him-away coffin.

Once Vin gets a full serving of Ariana Unplugged, he'll probably leave skid marks behind as he runs away.

Oreo pads into the room and then hops up on the end of my bed. Now that Mya's back to spending all her time at Milo's place, I'm sure she's feeling a little lonely.

"It's just us now, huh? Don't worry, I'll be sure to bring you back a treat from dinner."

She grumbles in satisfaction as I scratch behind her ears. Her black and white fur made her stand out immediately when I went to the shelter looking for a dog five years ago. She's some kind of Pomeranian mix and when they found her she'd clearly been abused.

For the first year I had her, she wouldn't bark at all, almost like she was scared to draw attention to herself. Remembering that time makes my throat feel like it's closing up. Oreo gave me someone to care for when I had no one else. This was right before I met Mya and back then I truly was all alone.

This adorable little pup saved my life just as much as I saved hers.

"I won't be out late. It's taking a little longer to get rid of this one. But he'll disappear just like all the others. Mama's bringing out the big guns tonight."

6

Din

PRESSURE IS A PART OF BUSINESS. WORKING WITH Fortune 500 companies and some of the wealthiest and most demanding people in the world have made me no stranger to thinking on my feet.

But tonight, *this date*, feels like the most critical interview of my life. My goal is to convince the most amazing woman I've ever met to give me a chance.

As I approach the restaurant, I look down at the navigation on my phone in confusion. There's a huge neon sign that looks like a pig right where...

Of course. My hand falls to my side before I glance down at the exquisitely tailored, hand-embroidered linen suit I'm wearing. Inwardly I groan. Andre is going to kill me if I ruin this. It's a sample from next season's line.

"You got me, my little troublemaker."

She's probably somewhere getting quite a kick out of the thought of me eating barbecue in a fancy suit. Little does she know I've eaten worse things while wearing fancy clothes. I can only wonder if she plans to laugh at my predicament from afar or if she even plans to show up tonight.

Nothing about this girl is predictable and even though I'm the target of her little prank, I can't deny I love it.

I see her coming and quickly school my expression into one of indifference. The quickest way to lose our little game is to let her know that anything she's done has actually gotten under my skin.

As she gets closer, my pulse elevates. Her long blond hair falls around her shoulders in natural waves and she appears to have no makeup on at all. Maybe she thought that would matter but seeing her barefaced just makes me want the same view on the pillow next to me tomorrow morning.

Her hazel eyes flash as she stops. "Here we are!"

"Yes. Here we are."

I was so focused on her laughing eyes that I hadn't had time to catalogue anything else about her appearance. But when she arches her back, pushing her chest out my attention is naturally drawn to the baby carrier on her chest.

Wait, she has a baby?

"You're a mom? I didn't realize. I mean, I p-probably should have asked."

There's no hiding my stammer and the triumphant look in her eyes tells me she's thrilled at finally cracking my resolve.

But I'm not that easily cowed and I actually like kids. Not that I expected her to bring a baby on our first date but we're already here. We might as well make the best of it.

"Who is this?" I lean closer to peer at the infant and she moves slightly so I can see.

Her movement shifts the child until his head pops out of the carrier like a jack-in-the-box. It has a scrunched up furry face and a mouth full of fangs.

"*Holy shit!*"

The people around us stop at my loud exclamation and I clap a hand over my mouth.

Ariana smiles prettily. "Everything okay?"

"Yes. Of course. I just meant to say... hello baby. What's his name?"

"This is Edward."

As she moves, the baby shifts in the carrier once again so even more of his face is visible. It looks like a gnarled cross between a wolf and a gremlin.

"You take him with you everywhere, hmm?"

"Not everywhere. Just around town. He's very good company."

"I'll bet. Let's go inside."

Her surprise is quickly covered with a bright smile. Interesting. So she didn't even think we'd make it inside. Part of me wants to ask how many men she's scared away with this demon baby trick. But I can't be the first one to open that door of conversation.

I want her to tell me.

More than that, I want her to *want* to tell me.

"There's no hostess or anything. You just find a seat." Ariana motions for me to follow along as she heads for a booth in the corner. Once we're seated she pulls her baby off her chest and sits him next to her.

I raise my hand to attract the attention of a passing waitress. "Yes, could we get a child seat please?"

She starts to say yes and then her eyes land on the doll next to Ariana. Then they swing back to me before she nods quickly and scurries off.

Ariana bursts out laughing.

"I'm glad you find this so amusing."

She shakes her head. "I should have guessed you'd just roll with it. Nothing seems to get to you."

She still doesn't get it. I'm just happy that she showed up. For the first time ever I'm excited about spending time with a woman. I know what she's trying to do with that demon doll. I saw her do it that first night at the bar too, with the salt. She's used to pushing people away and most men are too focused on themselves to notice or care why she's doing it.

But I'm not most men.

And I'm not going anywhere.

After the waitress comes back with a child booster seat, we settle into casual conversation. I can't say this is what I imagined our first date would look like but at least we're here.

And the view is incredible.

The waitress reappears at the side of the booth holding a tray of waters. She plunks a glass down in front of each of us unceremoniously before launching into a long explanation of the specials.

"I'll have the ribs platter."

"That sounds good, I'll have the same." I hand over the menu, hoping the waitress will clear out so I can have Ariana all to myself again.

What we eat isn't the reason why we're here. She looks nervous all of a sudden as the waitress gathers the unused menus from the table and leaves.

"So what do you think so far?" Ariana looks around the interior of the dark restaurant.

If the large outline of a pig on the sign outside wasn't enough of a clue, the inside has the same sign behind the bar. The tables are made from wood that looks like it's seen several centuries of use and even the menus have pigs all over them.

"It's cute. So many things in America seem to involve farm life. I love it."

Ariana stares back at me from across the scarred wooden table with fire in her eyes. Oh yes, she really thinks something as silly as a restaurant will scare me away. My girl doesn't know what she's up against.

That's how I already think of her. As my girl.

Women always think men are opposed to monogamy. What we're usually opposed to is boredom. I've listened to more than one female cousin lamenting the ex-boyfriend who broke up with her and ended up marrying someone else a year later.

He met the person who excited him. When that happens you cannot let her slip away.

Tonight is my shot and I don't think I'll get another. *Papa* used to tell us that only fate could have put a poor man like him in the path of a princess. Nicholas Lavin was a big believer in destiny guiding our paths.

Now I understand what he meant. When you meet the right woman, she rules your heart. Except my girl is more likely to rule the underworld.

A queen of darkness and mischief.

Much more my speed.

"You thought this would scare me off?"

"No. I just wanted to see if you could get a little messy."

"Why would you think I couldn't?"

"Seriously? You wore a cashmere sweater to the grocery store."

That makes me laugh.

"In my defense, my brother was giving me nothing but soup and crackers. He was basically starving me. I had to escape. I would have pulled on anything if it meant getting some real food."

That makes her relax a bit. Watching her walls come down little by little is a fascinating process. She has this way about her, as if she's braced for disappointment at all times.

It's probably second nature by now the way she deflects people's interest with sarcasm to keep them from getting too close. But then once she lets you in, it's like basking in the sun. The warmth of her attention makes me feel brand new.

"At least you have a brother to take care of you. I always wished I had a sibling. I mean, I have siblings but we didn't grow up together. So it's not the same."

"Maybe you wouldn't have wished for it if you'd seen how he tormented me when we were children. He once told me *La Befana* wouldn't bring me any presents if I didn't do exactly as he said. He had me hopping on one leg and howling like a wolf all day before our mother figured it out."

"*La Befana?*"

"In Italy, there are many different tales about her but in essence she's an old woman who brings gifts to the good children and leaves a lump of coal for the bad ones. Many people wander the streets dressed like her right after the New Year."

"It sounds like fun. I was always going back and forth between my parents for the holidays so I don't have that many fun memories. My dad was married several times before he met my mom so I mainly have memories of awkward family pictures with the half-siblings I don't know well."

"I'm sorry. That sounds pretty dismal."

"It was. But my roommate loves Christmas so I get a nice dose of Santa and his reindeer every year. That's something."

"Somehow I could see you being into Christmas. I think you like a little magic more than you let on."

She smiles and the sight punches me right in the chest.

"Tell me more about you. Anything."

Her smile falters slightly and I clear my throat. I have to remember not to come on too strong. She's been so adamant about not getting serious. If she knows how affected I am, she might walk out.

"Um, well you already know I'm a nurse. What do you do?"

"I work in fashion. I head the international division of a major fashion label. But I don't want to talk about work."

"Right. Let's not talk about work." She fiddles with the salt shaker on the table.

I have to think of something to get her to relax otherwise she's going to start pouring that salt and brewing a spell to get rid of me.

"So, who usually watches your son when you go out?"

That makes her smile. "He's usually unsupervised."

"That sounds a little irresponsible."

"Well, he enjoys his solitude. Like his mother."

"I can understand that. I enjoy my solitude as well. But every once in a while, it's nice to let someone in."

Our eyes meet and for a moment, I can see the same desire and longing I feel reflected back.

"I'm starting to see that."

"Ariana–"

She stands abruptly. "I have to go to the bathroom. I'll be back."

7

Ariana

I SPLASH A LITTLE BIT OF WATER ON MY FACE, TRYING to cool the flush in my cheeks. Why does he affect me more than anyone else? He's just a guy.

A gorgeous guy.

A guy who listens.

A guy who makes me want to see him again.

Thinking about it makes my hands shake. Would it really be the worst thing in the world to give a relationship a try?

Yes, the timing isn't great. But if anyone is aware of how fucked up this world can be, it's me. Bad things happen to good people and nothing ever turns out the way I hope.

Maybe this is my chance to take something for myself. To tell fate to shove it and that I'm going to grab the happiness I deserve. All he's asked for is to spend time with me. He's not a bum and he's definitely a decent person since he didn't wake me up for sex that first night we met.

What have I got to lose? If things don't work out between us then we'll just go our separate ways. No harm done.

I come back out of the bathroom with my mind made up. But when I get back to the table, Vin is gone. Deflated, I sink down into the booth.

"You must have finally scared him off, you little cock block," I mutter as Edward regards me with judgy eyes.

Then I see a crowd gathered around another table singing loudly. I sit on my knees in the booth to see better but it's not until someone moves that I see a familiar silhouette in the center of the melee. Vin is belting out Happy Birthday at the top of his lungs. Then he switches to singing in Italian to the delight of the crowd, who end the song with whistles and cheers.

Our waitress, the one who just a few minutes ago was completely disinterested, is now beaming at Vin like he's the answer to all of life's problems.

"I can't believe you just did that."

"Why? It's your birthday! Everyone should have a song on their birthday." He waves at everybody before coming back to our booth.

His eyes light up when he sees I'm back.

"There you are. I didn't want to start without you but it was a struggle. The food smells fantastic."

He gestures to the huge platters sitting in the middle of the table. The ribs special consists of a half rack with grilled corn, macaroni and cheese and bread on the side. Everything here is delicious and guaranteed to give you a heart attack at some point. Not exactly the kind of food I'd expect him to be into but then again, he's been surprising me every step of the way.

I settle back into my seat as he joins me.

"You have a nice voice."

"Thank you. I was just trying to put a smile on her face. Working on your birthday is no fun."

"No. It's not." The fact that he noticed someone else's unhappiness is exactly the kind of thing that makes him so different.

He's a genuinely good person. The kind that does the right thing because it's right and not for points.

The kind of guy worth taking a chance on.

As we eat, he asks more questions about my life. What I like to do when I'm not working, what my hobbies are, what I've been reading. Then he tells me about himself. He'll be twenty-six at his next birthday so he's almost exactly a year older. He loves his family, football (or what I call soccer) and hates spiders.

We discover that we have a lot of things in common, more than I would have guessed.

He hates to cook.

He enjoys decorating shows.

Edward didn't scare him off.

And that's the moment I realize I might be falling in love.

The time passes too quickly.

He's making a visible effort not to talk about anything heavy, I can tell, but he's not hiding his interest either. I guess he could tell his destiny speech might have scared me off earlier today so he's trying to keep things light. But nothing can disguise the burning intensity in his eyes when he looks at me.

After dinner we take our time poring over the dessert menu before deciding to get several to share. When Vin asks if I mind moving Edward so he can sit next to me, I find that I actually don't.

"I guess Edward can sit alone. Maybe I'll put him down for a little nap."

He smirks. "Lullabies always worked when I was his age."

"I'll keep that in mind."

After relocating Edward to the other side of the booth, Vin slides into the seat next to me. The booth that seemed so spacious only a few minutes ago has suddenly shrunk down to the size of a matchbox.

"That's better." He tucks a strand of hair behind my ear, his fingers lingering as they brush my cheek.

"Hi."

Suddenly shy about having him so close, my fingers twist around my napkin. I wouldn't have thought there was anything indecent about sharing a booth seat with a man but the way he's looking at me makes me feel naked.

It's unexpectedly intimate sharing the heat from his body. He smells crisp and clean like fresh air but something about it is completely unique to him. It makes me want to bury my face in his chest and take a deep breath.

"I've tried to be on my best behavior all night. But if you keep looking at me like that, I'm not sure I can be a gentleman."

"Who says I want you to be a gentleman?"

"You deserve gentleness," he replies. "You deserve a man who treats you like the queen you are."

"Maybe that's not what I need."

That brings out the fire in his eyes. He looks like he's close to taking a bite out of me as he leans closer.

"Tell me what you need then, my little devil. I'll make sure you have it. And I'll love giving it to you."

"Gentle can be good." I tap my bottom lip, loving how quickly his attention follows the motion. "But hard is better."

He clenches his teeth, the motion making his jaw work in a way I find insanely hot. He flexes his fingers on top of the table. I imagine that hand between my thighs.

I want that. I want that right here and now.

"Let me kiss you, *bella*. I'm not sure I'll survive if you don't."

At my shaky nod, his mouth is on mine like he can't wait another second for a taste. If I had any doubts that taking a chance on him was worth it, they all go up in flames as his tongue slides against mine. He kisses like he does everything else, with singular intensity and focus. The hand that was on the table slides behind my ear, holding my head in places as he devours me with long suctioning pulls. Every lick, every tug, every bite sends a pulse straight between my legs.

And that, ladies and gentleman, is how a kiss can make you wet enough to start a flood.

His hand trails down my neck and when it drops to my thigh, I whimper into his mouth. He swallows the soft sound and hums in response, like he's saying *don't worry, I'll make it better*.

He might as well have said *open sesame* because my thighs fall apart at the first touch. He curls just one finger and that's all it takes to make me shudder.

A loud ring makes him jerk back. Just that quickly, I remember we're in a public place. He looks like he's just had the same thought because he smiles sheepishly and pats his suit pocket.

"I apologize. I thought I turned my phone off."

"No, it's okay. You should check and make sure it's not important."

Being on your phone is considered bad date etiquette but Vin has been giving me his complete attention all night.

With a rueful smile, he draws his phone out of the inner pocket of his suit. He stares at the screen for a second and then mutters something in Italian.

"I am so sorry. I actually have to take this."

"Go ahead. I'll ask for the check. Then we can get out of here."

His eyes warm at my words before he leans over and plants a soft kiss on my forehead. Then he walks toward the back of the restaurant. He's probably going to take the call in the bathroom to get away from all the noise in here.

He's only gone a minute when the waitress comes by.

"How was everything? Do y'all need boxes?"

"Just the check, please."

"You got it." She glances over her shoulder as if looking for something. "Your friend is so nice. I couldn't believe it when one of the other girls told me who he is."

"Who he is?" I repeat slowly, trying to figure out what she means by that.

"I mean, he seems so normal." She chatters on as she gathers up the plates from our desserts and stacks them on her tray.

"I can totally see the resemblance now, of course. I mean, duh! He kinda looks like his brother. Do you think he'd mind taking a picture? I want to send it to my sister. She's the biggest Andre Lavin stan in the *world*. She won't believe this!"

My mind is spinning as she keeps talking. Andre Lavin. Anyone who is breathing and knows how to use social media knows who he is. But I *definitely* know who he is because he's all Mya can talk about lately. She's been working around the clock trying to land his business.

This is a huge deal and not something I can ignore. If Vin had been just a random guy, having a hot affair with him wouldn't be a big thing. He's sweet and intense but he's still a guy. Which means the chances of this thing working out in the long term are pretty low.

It was one thing to consider dating the hot guy with the intense eyes.

But it's a completely different thing to consider dating someone who is famous and rich and has the ability to wreck my best friend's career if things go south.

"Do you think you'll ever come by and bring Andre with you guys? I would love that so much. He is just everything."

I look up sharply. Oh geez, is the waitress *still* talking?

"Once you come back with the check, I'll find out if that might be possible. Okay?"

She beams. "Awesome! I'll go get that."

As soon as she turns around, I get up and grab Edward from the other side of the booth. Normally I'd feel guilty sticking a guy with the check but considering this guy is the spare heir to a billion dollar dynasty, I think it's okay.

I pause, then hurriedly take a pen out of my purse. I grab a napkin from the dispenser and write *I'm sorry*.

The thing is, I really am sorry things turned out this way. But that's what I get for thinking my luck had changed. It just took longer than usual for the universe to deliver its final kick in the teeth.

Outside, I walk a few blocks over before calling for an Uber. I'm sure when Vin sees that note he'll come running outside looking for me. But I can only hope we never run into each other again.

There's way too much at stake and I won't gamble on something this important. My best friend will win her client and life will go back to normal.

"Jesus, lady!"

A man walking by on the street jumps back with his hands held in the air. He glances at me and then back down to Edward before walking away quickly.

Well, I guess normal is relative. But I'll take it.

8

Din

OVER THE COURSE OF THE NEXT MONTH, I HAVE little time for regrets. I didn't earn my position through nepotism. Helming the international division of our company is more than a full-time job. I have to be up on what's trending in multiple countries all while convincing retailers worldwide that we're still the best of the best in menswear.

It's a demanding role and leaves little time for wondering what the hell I did that scared my fiery little devil away.

But in the random moments between department meetings and overseas calls, the thought of her sneaks in a time or two.

Or five.

"Is it just me or are these meetings getting longer?" Jason Gautier, the COO of the company, sits in front of my desk.

We just finished the most boring meeting of my life that consisted of charts, graphs and a scary amount of percentages.

Numbers aren't really my thing.

"I know. I'm glad I'm not an accountant."

"The math isn't the problem. I love numbers. Especially when they come with dollar signs in front of them. But when they're read in a monotone voice it's like taking an Ambien." Jason shakes his head like he's trying to get rid of all the information that was just rammed into our brains.

"Are we going out tonight?"

"Out? Out where?"

He tosses his pencil on my desk. "To a club. To a bar. Somewhere."

Nothing sounds less appealing to me right then. Being around a bunch of people who expect me to talk, laugh and drink the night away is not happening. For years, we've partied our way across the globe but there's a certain point where that gets old. My liver can't handle drinking all night and I'm beyond the point where I want to play Pussy Bingo at every club in the city.

"Maybe after I finish up here. If not, you guys go on without me."

He narrows his eyes. "What is up with you lately? You haven't been out with us in weeks."

"Work. Things are busy here."

"Yeah, I know. I work here too, asshole."

I'm not sure how he wants me to respond to that. Maybe if I ignore him long enough he'll get the hell out of my office. I turn back to my computer and start reading emails.

"Fine. Be like that. Go home and climb in bed with a cup of tea. Or whatever."

I ignore him until I hear the sound of my office door close behind him. I haven't been going home to a cup of tea, for fuck's sake.

I've been out.

Okay, maybe I've been spending more time than usual hanging out in the bar at the Fitz but that's only because I like their vodka tonics. And the grumpy ass bartender. His face looks like how I feel.

"That doesn't sound like him."

"I know. That's why I have no idea what to do."

"I'll take care of it. Can you talk to the staff? Maybe keep everyone away until I can figure out what's going on."

"You got it, boss."

The voices outside my door aren't even trying to keep it down.

"I can hear you out there!" I yell.

Andre opens the door and pokes his head in. *"Dio,* this is even worse than I thought."

"Go away. I'm not in the mood." I swivel in my chair to give him my back.

Undeterred, he comes in and closes the door. Clearly he doesn't care if I'm not happy to see him. Then again, we're brothers. This isn't the first time we've had a fight, verbal or physical, and it won't be the last. It's probably better for me to take out my frustration on him than anyone else.

"You're in a mood. What's going on?"

"Nothing is going on. Jason just gossips like a little girl."

The closer he gets, the more I notice the strain around his eyes. I've been so preoccupied with my own situation that I've clearly been missing some things.

"What's going on with you? How is the marketing campaign going?"

"I thought branching out into the bridal market was the right move. But sometimes I wonder. What if I'm wrong? It's a lot of money to gamble. And if it isn't successful..."

All at once, his shoulders drop and he seems to deflate right in front of my eyes. My brother is known for keeping his cool in every situation, which makes this all the more strange. The idea of the always elegant, unflappable Andre struggling with insecurity is shocking.

It also isn't as satisfying as I would have thought it would be. It doesn't make me feel bigger to see him brought down. Instead I'm ashamed of the thoughts I've had lately. We're brothers. Partners. Jealousy has no place here. Nothing comes before family.

"Tell me how I can help, *fratellone*."

He shakes his head and looks out the picture window behind me. I turn so I can see what has his attention but it's just a view of the city streets below, the cars and people like toys on a game board.

"All those people rushing to go nowhere," he murmurs. "Only to turn around the next day and do it all over again."

Hearing such sentiments from him is unexpected. I've always been the more philosophical of the two of us. Andre is more practical. All of his passion and creativity goes into his designs. I've never heard him talk like this.

We sit in silence for a moment, watching the flow of the world on the streets below. Observing people from a distance really puts things in perspective. It's hard not to feel like we're all just chess pieces in a larger game.

"Do you remember what *Papa* used to say about how life is a puzzle?" I ask him.

"Love is the missing piece," we both chant the words together.

"I miss him."

He nods. "Me too."

"He's proud of us, isn't he?"

Andre sighs. "I hope so."

After Andre leaves, I pull open the top drawer of my desk and pull out the napkin Ariana left. The *I'm sorry* seems like it's gotten darker and more aggressive in the time since it was written, like the words are mocking me.

I only wish I'd ended that phone call fast enough to catch her on the way out. All it would have taken was a conversation to figure out what went wrong. Although I have a bit of a clue because the waitress had come back with the check and immediately asked for an autograph.

Then she asked if I planned to bring Andre by.

None of it makes any sense. Did Ariana think I was lying by not telling her my last name? She didn't seem like the type who would care about fame or money.

Frustrated, I toss the napkin back in the drawer. It's messing with me more than I care to admit. Maybe it's my conversation with Andre, all that talk about puzzle pieces.

Our father was a true romantic. The kind that trusted his heart over facts and believed there was a guiding hand behind everything.

Despite being raised by a man that could teach a course on romance, neither of his sons seem to have inherited that gene.

Maybe because it just didn't make any fucking sense.

There are billions of people on the earth so how can anyone hope to find *The One*? What if you take a wrong turn and miss your soul mate? What does that mean? That you'll die alone?

What God would devise such a system?

But then I think of Ariana out there somewhere living her life. I imagine her marching through the city with Edward strapped to her chest, looking for some trouble to get into.

Maybe she's not *The One*. But she's the only one I want. So nothing else really matters.

Frustrated, I run a hand through my hair. If she doesn't want to see me there's nothing I can do about that. And I'm too busy to spend time sulking. Before we started this company, Andre and I made a promise to give it our all.

The Lavin brand is our number one priority and nothing will ever get in the way of that.

So as angry as I am, I make a conscious decision to let it go.

I turn to the window and gaze out at the fading light. The sun is setting, gilding everything on the horizon with hues of crimson and gold. It reminds me that no matter what happens, the world keeps turning and life goes on. But that doesn't mean I can't ask for a little help.

"*Papa.* Help me. If she is my missing piece, then guide her back to me."

II

HOW IT'S GOING

9

Ariana

Two Years Later...

ALL GOOD THINGS COME TO AN END. AS I TAKE another gulp of champagne, I mentally calculate how long I have until all the shit hits the fan.

Les Printemps is a fancy French restaurant that is perfect for a fancy ass engagement party. Tonight it's been decorated with cream and silver streamers to match the wedding party colors. The flowers will be either white roses or calla lilies and all the bridesmaids will wear peach dresses.

How do I know all of this?

Because I have somehow found myself smack dab in the middle of the wedding of the century.

When Mya worked things out with Happy Hour Hottie, I was thrilled for her but sad for myself. I envisioned coming home to a cold, dark apartment and eating meals alone each night. But just like always, Mya looked out for me.

When her firm hired a new receptionist, she somehow convinced her that I would be a great roommate. Casey turned out to be not only a sweet person but also a close friend. Mya always jokes that she brought me a "Bonus Bestie".

She doesn't realize that she also put me on a collision course straight back to the man I've been avoiding for two years now.

"What's your name, dear?"

I'm sitting at one of the tables at the back of the private room, hoping no one will notice I'm here. The older couple sitting on the opposite side has apparently decided it's time to make polite small talk.

I am not going to survive an entire night of this.

"I'm Ariana. Hi."

They introduce themselves but I can't hear them that well so I just nod politely.

"How do you know the happy couple?" the woman trills.

"Oh you know. The usual." Then I whisper, "*Threesome.*"

The wife gasps and then gets up to move to another table. The husband lingers until his wife notices he's not at her side. "Henry!"

He scrambles out of his seat, leaving me at the table alone.

"Ari! What are you doing all the way back here? You're supposed to be up front." Casey grabs my hand and pulls me up.

I follow her to the tables closer to the door. People are just starting to show up, which means I'm running out of time.

"Let's go to the bathroom. I need to fix my hair."

Casey follows as I weave my way through tables toward the other side of the room. There's a short hallway that leads to the sumptuously outfitted ladies room.

Casey plops down on the velvet chaise against the wall. Her dark hair is smoothed back into an elegant low bun. I make a big show of fixing my hair in the mirror.

"I'm just a girl from Gracewell, Virginia but I'm wearing a thousand dollar cocktail dress and about to dance all night at my engagement party."

"You look beautiful. And your future husband is hot."

"Is this really my life? Just pinch me now so I can be sure I'm not dreaming. Am I seriously marrying Andre Lavin?"

I pinch her arm lightly making her laugh. But I'm dying inside. Because her dream is my nightmare.

The one man I went out of my way to avoid is going to come crashing back into my life tonight.

When Casey first told me she was secretly seeing one of Mya's biggest clients, I hadn't thought it would matter. She was mainly worried about getting fired.

I hadn't had the heart to tell her a man like Andre Lavin would likely lose interest before anyone at work had time to find out about the affair.

But once again, the universe had the last laugh. Andre adores Casey and would walk through fire to keep her in his life. Which means that from the moment he proposed, I've had a big ole' countdown clock running in the back of my mind.

T minus whatever until Vin figures out exactly who I am.

Mya bursts into the room followed by Anya Petrova, another one of their coworkers. Both squeal appreciatively at the sight of Casey in her fitted black bandage dress. It's from some exclusive designer friend of Andre's and looks like it was made just for her.

Which it probably was.

Mya looks in the mirror behind us. "Andre just arrived. Why didn't you guys come together?" She fixes a few tendrils of hair that have come loose from her long black braid. Her eyes are bright and her cinnamon skin tone is radiant.

She has the same glow that Casey has.

Good sex with a man who adores you is clearly great for the complexion. And yes, I'm a little jealous.

"He had to do something for his mom. Also, his brother wanted to talk to him about some investment thing. I told him I'd meet him here."

Anya hops up on the counter and crosses her legs. We don't know each other that well but she's always been a funny addition to our Girl's Night. Her dark hair is cut into a razor-sharp bob that emphasizes her blue eyes.

"I'm still trying to decide if I'm mad at you for not introducing me to that brother," she says.

Casey turns with a frown. "Philippe?"

"If he's the tall dark and yummy guy who looks just like Andre, then yes."

"He *doesn't* look just like Andre."

They all turn to stare at me. "I mean... no one looks exactly like someone else. Unless they're twins. Even then."

Mya regards me for a long moment. "*Riiiiight.* Anyway, I'm not sure how you missed him, Anya. He's been to at least a few of the marketing meetings. Maybe Casey can hook you up."

Anya grimaces. "I'm just kidding around, guys. I have a boyfriend. Kind of. It's complicated."

"Well, if the guy you're with won't commit, there's nothing wrong with looking," Casey says. "Maybe you two will hit it off and we'll end up being sisters-in-law."

"I don't know about that but I won't say no to an introduction. Share the eye candy, girl." Anya winks.

"Come on, let's go find him." Casey says.

"Right now?" I ask, frantically trying to think of a reason we need to stay in the bathroom.

Preferably all night.

Casey grabs Anya's hand and tugs her off the counter. "No time like the present. Let's get this party started!"

They all whoop and start for the door. I follow behind feeling like I'm on my way to an execution. It's almost eight o'clock and the party will start soon. Then my time will officially be up.

I've known this moment was coming ever since Casey came home with an engagement ring on her finger the size of an aircraft carrier. But now that it's here, I'm not only nervous but worried.

The last thing I want is for him to make a scene and ruin Casey's party.

Before I reach the door, Mya steps in front of me. "What is going on with you?"

"I have no idea what you're talking about."

"You're being so weird lately. What was all that stuff about twins?"

"Nothing. I was just saying...it doesn't matter. This night is about Casey. We need to go out there and support her. You know, just in case any of Andre's rich friends are mean to her."

"No one is going to be mean to her. Andre will be glued to her side all night."

"That's true. But you know, I'm just getting mentally ready. You should always be prepared to slap a bitch, just in case."

She moves aside so I can pass but I can tell she's not entirely convinced. Which means if I plan on keeping my little escapade with the groom's brother under wraps, I need to watch my step tonight.

And my mouth.

As soon as we enter the private room reserved for the party, Mya is pulled into a conversation with someone I don't know. I take the opportunity to stake out the room.

In one corner we have a few of Casey's friends from home. I recognize one of the girls from Instagram.

Then near the buffet are several Mirage Agency employees. Casey's old boss, James Lawson, just put what looks like pâté on his plate. He swipes a cracker through it and takes a small bite before making a face.

He's definitely going for burgers after this is over.

I circulate for about half an hour, sticking to the edge of the crowd. The room is full with quite a few older people. These must be relatives of Andre's. Still no sign of Vin.

I grab a glass of champagne from a passing waiter and take a miniscule sip. Maybe if I just keep moving I can avoid him for one more day.

Then I turn around.

He's right behind me. Our eyes meet and his hand that was in the process of lifting a glass of champagne pauses.

He blinks twice. "*Ariana?*"

I gulp. "Hey."

His eyes narrow at the casual greeting. But before he can say anything else, Casey and Andre appear next to us.

"Oh, you already met!" Casey looks between us with a big smile.

It's obvious she's been drinking because she gets even more cheerful when she's had a few.

"We just started talking. I would love for you to introduce us," Vin says smoothly.

His grin makes me want to punch him. Only someone who knows our history would catch how carefully he's crafting his sentences. He didn't say that we'd just *met*. Only that we'd just started *talking*.

"This is Ariana Silva. Ari, this is Andre's little brother, Philippe."

"How do you guys know each other?" Vin tilts his head mockingly.

"We–"

But Casey is chattering away before I have a chance to deflect.

"Ari is my roommate! I mean she was, before I moved into the penthouse with Andre."

"Is that right?"

"Yes. I loved living there. I still miss it. I miss you. I miss Oreo." Casey wraps her arms around me and I can't help returning the hug. She's so happy it's contagious.

Vin watches me the entire time.

"Oreo?" he asks lightly.

"Her dog! She's the cutest thing, you have to see!" Casey pulls out her phone and starts sliding through her pictures.

I close my eyes. "I'm sure he – I'm sorry, what was your name again?"

Vin's jaw moves slightly, the only sign that he's bothered. "Philippe Lavin. My friends call me Vin."

"Well, Vin. I'm sure you don't want to see pictures of my dog."

"I love dogs. Besides, it'll be good to get to know you better. We're going to be working so closely these next few weeks."

"We are?"

"Of course." He smiles down at Casey. "Your friend has already agreed to help me plan the bachelor party."

This conversation is making my head hurt. "Wait, I agreed to do what now? Why would I be planning the bachelor party?"

Vin's smile spreads even wider. "It's actually a joint bachelor and bachelorette party. Since Andre insists on not being separated from his true love for even one night."

His words are kind but the saccharine sweet way he's speaking tells me exactly what he thinks of that idea.

Casey grins up at Andre. "Your brother is so jealous. He just wants to make sure I don't have a stripper."

Andre scowls. "You don't need a stripper. I'll strip for you."

Vin ignores them. "Since the parties have to be at the same time and at least partially overlap, we have to plan them together."

Casey nods. "He's the best man. And you're the maid of honor."

"That's right," Vin singsongs. "Casey, since you have your phone out, can you send me Ariana's info? You know, for the planning."

It's my turn to narrow my eyes.

"Of course. I'll text it to you, Philippe." Casey starts typing and then takes a deep breath. "We're so lucky to have you guys helping us. So many details."

"You don't have to worry about anything except making my brother the happiest guy alive. Ariana and I will take care of everything."

Casey and Andre drift away to mingle with the other guests. I try to follow but Vin moves so he's in my way. There's not much I can do without causing a scene and I'm not going to make a mad dash for the door in front of all these people. Especially not wearing heels.

"Have you put any spells on anyone lately?"

I shake my head, not willing to be drawn into our old chemistry. It's been two years and yet he still has this pull that makes me want to jump in his arms. It's infuriating. Especially when he doesn't seem all that bothered by the fact that I'm here. It's more like he's amused at the turn of events. Worse, it feels like he's laughing at me.

"You look beautiful, Ariana. You have roses in your cheeks when you're pissed off."

My hands rise to the sides of my face automatically. "It's hot in here. That's all."

He hums in agreement and the sound instantly takes me back to that night. That perfect, insane, bonkers first date. And the full intensity of what I gave up hits me with so much force I feel lightheaded.

"I really should go. You know, mingle."

"Of course. I'll text you when I can meet to start planning."

He doesn't say anything else and I shift uncomfortably from foot to foot. "That's it?"

"What else is there? We're nothing more than strangers, right?"

When he walks off, I'm left standing alone and feeling incredibly small.

He doesn't text me that night. Or the next morning.

But I do have three voicemails from my parents. I groan as I hit the button to play them. I might as well get it over with.

Daddy Warbucks: Why is your mother saying she needs money for a plane ticket? The woman already takes half my money every month!

I roll my eyes. My father has only gotten exponentially more wealthy since he divorced my mother when I was twelve. So there's no way my mom is getting half of his money. A fact my mom loves to rant about because apparently if she'd waited a few years to divorce him she could have gotten even more alimony than the ridiculous amount she gets now.

Daddy Warbucks: Is the money really for you? Mija, if you need money you can always ask–

MESSAGE DELETED

Drama Mama: I got your messages, darling. I'll be there in plenty of time for your little appointment. Your father, of course, had to waste my time on the phone before buying the ticket. Can you believe his nerve–

MESSAGE DELETED

Daddy Warbucks: I forgot to ask. Don't you have something medical coming up soon? Let me know if you need a check–

MESSAGE DELETED

I get out of bed and shuffle into the bathroom. One hot shower later, I'm dressed in some leggings and a sweatshirt and ready to start my day. My shift isn't until this evening so I plan to clean up a little and get some grocery shopping done.

Still no texts.

My disappointment at not hearing from him makes no sense. He's right. We are strangers now. I was the one who insisted on it. Why does it bother me that he seems oblivious to seeing me again?

Maybe because I'd built this moment up in my head expecting fireworks and instead only got a lukewarm fizzle. I've spent so much time worrying and wondering how he'd react to seeing me again and the reality is that he doesn't care. The time we spent together clearly wasn't as memorable for him.

Which does not hurt my feelings.

But it does make me angry.

Despite how it ended, we were ... something to each other. I guess he thinks it's funny to act like we never knew each other at all. This whole thing seems to be a game to him.

He's volunteering my time to help plan parties and smirking at me like I'm the one who once pursued him.

Well, I have something to fix that. Maybe he needs a little reminder of exactly who he's dealing with.

I send a quick text to Casey for the information I need before I start putting together a little surprise for him. Vin wants us to plan the bachelor and bachelorette parties, does he?

Well, I'll give him a little preview of what he can expect.

10

Din

A FEW DAYS LATER, I'M ON A VIDEO CALL WITH Andre, Jason and the company's creative director.

I've finally convinced Andre it's time for the company to introduce a line of ready-to-wear suits. It took a lot of convincing. When my brother hears the words *off-the-rack* he imagines ill-fitting, cheap imitations of what a suit should be.

But I have a vision of something better. With my brother's signature style, we could bring elegance to a new demographic and introduce a new line of revenue at the same time.

My assistant comes in. She's holding a bunch of mail and a large box.

When Andre first decided to open a permanent office in DC, we both went through a carousel of assistants until we were able to weed out the fortune hunters, undercover gossip reporters and the ones who were just plain incompetent.

I hit the jackpot when I found Cheryl Robins. The older black woman is a mother of three, grandmother of five and guards my office like a mother hen. She also makes a mean cup of coffee and has a no-nonsense demeanor that keeps me in line.

She's been married to her high school sweetheart for the past thirty years otherwise I would have gotten down on one knee and proposed by now.

"Mr. Lavin. You have a package."

When she sees that I'm on a call, she puts a finger to her lips and then places the mail carefully on the edge of the desk within my reach. I wave as she tiptoes out.

I almost want to tell her not to bother. It's not like I'm paying attention in this meeting anyway. I should be. This is my pet project.

But instead my mind is on the engagement party.

Ariana.

The woman who has haunted my dreams for the past two years. I was angry at first, of course. Part of that was ego. What man wants to be left on a date without a word?

That's just rude.

But underneath the surface level anger, I'd been hurt. The connection I'd felt to her instantly was unlike anything I'd ever experienced. It's the kind of thing you can't understand unless you've met someone who knocks you on your ass from day one.

But as the months went by, I kept my promise to myself. I wasn't pining away for her. I lived my life with the dial set to maximum. There wasn't an opportunity I'd left unexplored or a moment I'd let go to waste. Our business has only grown and increased its market share. I'm proud of the life I've built and yes, I've dated here and there.

And all of it didn't mean a damn the moment I saw her again.

Underneath it all, that thing that connects us is still there. She was frosty, no doubt expecting me to call her out for ghosting me. However, time has dulled my anger and brought me to a new understanding. Despite what happened in the past, today is a new day. And each new day is another chance to show her how good we could be together.

It's so fun to watch heat climb her cheeks every time I pay her a compliment. Or every time I piss her off. Both are amusing.

Planning this joint bachelor party is going to be very interesting, that's for sure.

With a sigh, I pick up the box on the top of the pile of mail. I use my letter opener to slit the tape holding the box closed. There's white paper taped over the contents. As soon as I peel back the tape, the contents explode upward, a volley of bright shapes springing in every direction.

"What the–"

I touch my nose gingerly where one of the plastic things hit the tip. My desk is now covered in glitter and on the floor... are those what I think they are? I lean down to pick up the item that hit me in the nose.

When I stand back up, I'm holding a large red dildo.

"Philippe, what was that?"

"Are you okay?"

"*Is that a—*"

I slap at the keyboard frantically to end the meeting. The screen freezes for a second, showing several confused faces.

Leaning down, I grab at the brightly colored penises all over the floor. After a minute, I line them all up on my desk. There are about ten in total, some smaller and probably novelty items while there are a few big ones with controls that actually look functional.

All at once, I lose it.

Just imagining how the executives in our company reacted to seeing me get hit with a dick bomb makes me laugh until my sides hurt. I'm still wiping away tears of laughter when Cheryl comes in again. She looks at my messy desk in confusion.

"Is everything all right, Mr. Lavin? I heard something—" She halts when her eyes land on the array of pleasure poles on my desk.

"I just got a delivery from a friend. It's ... a modern art display from a new European artist. Quite provocative, isn't it?"

She puts a hand to her chest. "It is very striking.

As soon as the door closes behind her I fall back in my chair laughing again.

Well played, my little devil.

Ariana loves to do these strange things but she's not fooling me. The woman I talked to in the bar wasn't flighty or ditzy at all. She was insightful and thoughtful and had a shadow in her eyes that told me she'd been disappointed by people more often than not. She's a warm, caring woman who is afraid of letting anyone too close.

"Still trying to scare me off, hmm?"

She's so used to people backing away that I don't think she has any idea what to do with someone who challenges her. But her smart mouth doesn't turn me off a bit. In fact, I enjoy the hell out of waiting to see what wild thing she'll do next.

And I think she feels the same even if she can't admit it.

Well, let's not disappoint her.

I crack up again as I look at all the penises on my desk. She really outdid herself finding a wide variety of shapes, colors and sizes. It's a funny mental image to think of her poring over some sketchy website to buy all of these. Unless she already had them on hand.

Which, knowing Ariana, is not out of the realm of possibility. In her mind having a bunch of dildos for *just in case* probably isn't that weird.

It takes me a few tries but I manage to get a good picture that has all of the dildos in frame. Lined up in rows on my desk they look like a pornographic candyland.

I text her the picture and then think long and hard about what to write.

Vin: Thank you for the thoughtful gift. You can never have too many.

Later that night, I check my phone again, amused I still haven't gotten a response.

Could it be that I have finally surprised her? Maybe she thought the dick explosion would be the thing that won the war.

It's tempting to think she might have finally given up on this feud but I know my girl well enough not to rest easy. Ariana is not the type to allow me to have the last word. Which only means she's formulating some new evil plan to take me down.

I am undeniably looking forward to it.

But first, it's my turn.

It's tempting to go all out and buy something extravagant but instinct tells me that's the wrong move. She doesn't want to be impressed. That's the whole point here.

All I can do is be sincere.

I order three dozen roses to be delivered to her address. Maybe she'll enjoy them. Maybe she'll throw them in the trash. I can only hope they give her a little bit of joy. She deserves that even if she's convinced it's not what she wants.

Plus, I'll enjoy seeing what she decides. I've given her enough time to stew.

I'm going to go see my girl tomorrow.

11

Ariana

DESPITE GETTING AT LEAST SIX HOURS OF SLEEP, I still feel exhausted. One of the downsides of working part-time is not having a set schedule. I fill in where needed, sometimes going back and forth between day and night shift.

The agency messed up my schedule, so I'm not on shift again until next week. Which is the perfect opportunity for me to do a little sprucing up. I enjoy redecorating. It makes me feel like I'm starting over with a clean slate.

A clean slate would be nice. Yesterday I expected an angry phone call from Vin or maybe a retaliatory flaming bag of shit.

Instead he'd sent that tongue-in-cheek message that made me feel petty as hell. Clearly he's not holding a grudge. So that just leaves me as the asshole who can't let the past go.

In our game of wits, he's definitely winning.

Which, of course, *really* pisses me off.

I call my mom and leave her a message. She never told me exactly when she'd be arriving but it should be this afternoon. Then I change into an old pair of gym shorts and one of my favorite science shirts. This one says *Higgs Boson Gives Me A Hadron*.

It's incredibly geeky and always puts a smile on my face.

An hour later, I'm in the middle of rearranging the pictures on the wall when the front door opens with no warning. The couch is sitting in the middle of the floor blocking my escape route so I clutch the level in my hand like a weapon. Then Casey pokes her head in, looking both ways, before she enters.

"It's safe!" she calls over her shoulder.

"Are you sure?" Mya's voice echoes in from the hallway.

Casey glances at me. "You're not doing anything weird in here, are you?"

I scowl.

She shrugs. "I had to ask."

Mya follows her inside. "See, I told you. I knew it was bad. It's always bad when she starts moving the furniture around."

"What are you guys doing here?"

"This is an intervention!" Casey holds up a finger for emphasis.

"Oh dear god."

I give up on the pictures and throw the level onto the couch. I contemplate moving it back so they can sit and then decide it can stay. Maybe if they have to sit at an awkward angle in the middle of the floor they'll go away. I head into the kitchen.

"Wait, where are you going?" Casey asks. She kneels to pet Oreo who has come padding out of the bedroom at the sound of voices.

"This situation requires coffee."

Mya takes a seat at the kitchen island. While the coffee is brewing, I grab a bag of chips for her and then stand on tiptoe to reach the top cabinet for the gross little pecan wheel thingies Casey likes to snack on.

"You've been busy," Mya comments looking around the room.

"*Hello, Ariana. How have you been? You look ravishing as always,*" I say in a high-pitched voice.

"Is that supposed to be me?" Mya snickers.

"No, that's Casey. You're more like this," I clear my throat and lower my voice. "*Bitch, why is this room so messy?*"

Mya laughs. "Do I have laryngitis?"

Casey crosses her arms. "This is serious. We're worried about you. You haven't been yourself lately."

"By that she means you've been really quiet and well-behaved," Mya chimes in.

"I'm fine, guys. No intervention needed." I pour myself a cup of coffee and inhale the orgasmic scent. "This is the only thing I need right here."

Mya takes a chip from the bag and eats it with a loud crunch.

"You've been weird since the engagement party. Don't try to deny it. You barely said two words all night."

I take a long bracing sip of coffee. They both stare expectantly. I sigh. Clearly they aren't going away.

"Maybe it's not so easy to be around all these happy couples. Did you ever think of that? Everyone is pairing off. You've got Happy Hour Hottie. Casey's with Mr. Instagram."

Casey looks devastated. "Oh my god. We should have realized–"

Mya scoffs. "Ariana. You expect me to believe that crap?"

"*Mya*! She's pouring out her feelings here." Casey crosses her arms.

She's so adorable.

"I'm just kidding. Guys, nothing is wrong. I'm just horny. I need to get laid."

"There it is," Mya waves her hand triumphantly.

Casey looks disappointed.

Mya crunches another chip. "Okay, things are starting to make sense. But why haven't you taken care of the problem, Oh Queen of Dildo Land?"

I snicker to myself. I have always maintained an impressive sex toy collection. But that's not the point.

"You two don't understand because you've got good dick available when you need it. But sometimes there's no substitute for the real thing. Some of us are in a drought, okay? It's not fair to brag about your sex storms while I'm dying of thirst!"

"That metaphor makes no sense." Mya crunches another chip.

"I should have come back to visit more," Casey laments. "I've been such a bad friend. You're here all alone."

"Yes, I'm a pathetic spinster," I say drily.

"Oh no, that's not what I meant!"

Mya laughs. "She's trolling you, Casey. Ariana doesn't care about getting married. She's going to live to one hundred and still be fabulous as hell and buy our kids really expensive, noisy presents."

"And don't you forget it."

Mya gets up then, but not before taking a few more chips from the bag. She gives both of us a hug.

"I've got to run. Now that we know you aren't dying, I have to get back to work."

My heart sinks down to my knees at her words. I smile weakly. "Not dying."

Casey takes her seat at the counter after Mya leaves. She watches quietly as I clean up the chips Mya left all over the counter.

"I should be asking how *you* are doing? Are you getting excited? Nervous? The big day will be here before you know it."

Casey clasps her hands together in excitement. "I know! I can't wait to see my dress. Andre is putting the final touches on it now."

"Comes in handy to be marrying one of the hottest designers in the world, huh?"

Her eyes soften. "I'd marry that man in a potato sack."

"I really am happy for you."

She squeezes my hand. "I want you to be happy, too. Maybe I can hook you up. Andre has so many friends."

"No blind dates."

"Come on, it'll be fun. We're already hosting a dinner this weekend just so I can invite Philippe and Anya over at the same time. Playing Cupid is so much fun."

The mug I'm holding slips from my fingers and shatters right at my feet.

"Oh no. Don't move. I'll get the mop."

While Casey is gone, my mind turns over her words. She's fixing up Anya and Vin this weekend?

It doesn't matter, remember?

He's not your boyfriend.

He's not your anything.

I sigh heavily. After I sent him a package of weaponized penises, we're probably not even friends. Maybe he'll like being set up with Anya. She's pretty and will be happy to go out on dates with him.

She doesn't have to measure her life in between cancer screenings either.

Casey comes back with the mop. I pick up the pieces of the broken mug carefully, depositing the broken shards in the trash, before mopping up the coffee on the floor.

There's a knock at the door.

"Can you get that?"

Casey hands me the broom. "Sure. I actually need to get ready to leave anyway."

The door slams a minute later and I hear her come back.

"Who was it?"

"Flower delivery. These are so pretty."

I turn to see a huge bouquet of roses on the counter.

"Who are they from?"

Casey shrugs. "There's no card. Maybe you have a secret admirer."

I smile weakly. "It's probably just my mom. She's planning to visit soon."

As soon as Casey turns to go back into the living room, I scowl at the flowers. Vin really thinks he's so clever. My cheeks warm remembering how he'd said I had roses in my cheeks. Clearly the penises haven't deterred him at all.

Which is a terrifying thought.

But the reasons I pushed him away two years ago are no longer valid. Mya has an established working relationship with the Lavin brand now. They trust her and she delivers every time. They wouldn't drop her company just because I had a relationship with Vin, even if things didn't work out.

Plus, I'm almost at the point where I can trust that I have a future to spend with someone.

When I was first diagnosed with breast cancer, it was seven years ago. I was partying my way through college without a care in the world.

Imagine my surprise when a routine doctor's visit turned up a small lump in my right breast.

I followed every one of my doctor's orders. I underwent a lumpectomy and met with my doctor every three months after that. I was sure that if I followed the rules my brush with cancer would be a distant memory. Because that's how things work, right? You follow the Yellow Brick Road until you reach the end.

I'd been going to my cancer screenings for two years when a routine scan found another tumor.

Any hope I'd had that cancer was done with me died that day. I was told by my doctors that I was lucky. Due to its location, my new oncologist thought it was a piece of the original tumor that got left behind. The tumor was so small and because we'd caught it early, my prognosis was excellent. But hearing the words *it's back* from your oncologist doesn't make you feel lucky.

I was terrified.

But it was also a wakeup call. I got serious about finishing school, switching my major from Sociology to Nursing. Overnight I went from party girl to serious student.

From optimist to realist.

I've lived each day since then fully aware that it could come back again. Keeping men at arm's length was easier than having to explain what my appointments are for or answering questions about my scar. Then I'd have to deal with the pity or even worse, the guy who would stay with you just because he feels bad about leaving the "girl who had cancer".

I'm happier alone, living each day as it comes. Planning a future feels like tempting fate to knock me down once more.

Vin is the first man I've met who makes me want to take a chance. He won't pity me because of what I've been through. I smile. No, he'd probably tell me to make cancer my bitch.

And something tells me that if fate knocks me down, he'll be right there to catch me.

"Ari, did you hear me?"

When I look up, Casey is standing right in front of me. It's obvious by the way she's waving her hands around she's been trying to get my attention for a while.

These damn roses are throwing me off.

"I'm sorry. I'm a little distracted."

"It's okay. We probably shouldn't have just barged in like that. You're really okay?"

"I'm really okay. Quick, let's hug before I change my mind." I open my arms.

Casey laughs but gives me a quick squeeze. Although we like to tease her about being too nice for her own good, I love that Casey is so sweet. She's the mother hen of our group clucking over us all worriedly. It's a nice feeling to have someone care about whether I'm okay.

She's more maternal than the mother who actually gave birth to me.

"Okay, I'm going to go. Andre should be back home now. We still need to make some final adjustments to the seating chart."

"Kiss that handsome man of yours for me."

"Maybe I'll kiss more than that."

As she walks out I yell, "Rub it in, why don't ya?"

I've just finished moving the furniture back into position when there's another knock at the door.

What is it with today? It's like Union Station in here. I swear if Casey has come back for more tough love I'm going to shove her cute little body down the stairs.

I snatch the door open. "Aren't you supposed to be sucking–"

Vin shifts the brown paper bags in his arms. A large cardboard box rests at his feet.

"Please finish that sentence. I can't take the suspense."

Before I can answer, he pushes the box with his foot and I'm forced to move back or let him run over my toes. After pushing the box next to the couch, he looks around like he's taking note of the layout.

"Nice place." He heads for the kitchen.

Oreo pokes her head around the island and then shrinks back when she sees an unfamiliar face.

"She's black and white. Like the cookie." Vin chuckles before kneeling and snapping his fingers gently. "*Ciao, piccolina.*"

Oreo runs back to my room.

"She's not fond of strangers," I comment.

He hums. "Neither is her mother."

"What are you doing here?"

He glances over his shoulder. "You hate cooking. So I brought takeout."

He shrugs out of his suit jacket and hangs it on the back of one of the bar stools. Then, as if he's been here a million times before, starts opening cabinets and taking down plates and glasses.

"Make yourself at home," I mutter.

"I brought Chinese and Mexican. Pick your pleasure."

His choice of words is just begging for a comment but I can tell by the smirk on his face that he's hoping I take the bait.

Pick my pleasure, huh?

Why don't you put yourself on a plate and let me taste that?

Instead I open the first bag and start pulling out containers. The fragrant smells make my mouth water instantly.

"Chinese or Mexican? How do I choose?"

"Let's go with all of the above," Vin suggests. He pushes a container of enchiladas across the counter to me before sticking some chopsticks into a carton of Lo Mein.

"That sounds good to me." I snag an eggroll from the open container so I can get a taste before they start to get soggy.

"Not that I'm complaining but you still haven't told me why you're here. And *how* you're here? How did you get my address?"

He slurps up a noodle before reaching for the eggrolls. "I have my ways."

"You're such a stalker."

He hesitates. "When Casey sent me your info, she sent me the contact she has for you in her phone. Name, address, phone number, email address–"

"Okay, I get the picture. Now you have everything you need to steal my identity. Great."

He laughs. "That's not what I want from you."

"No comment."

"You're no fun. Where's the girl who brought a demon baby on our first date?"

I freeze with a mouthful of enchilada. We still haven't talked about what happened. Talk about an elephant in the room.

We chew in silence for a minute before I put the enchilada down on my plate.

"I really am sorry about leaving like that. Mya had just started competing for the Lavin account at work. It was such a big deal for her. When I found out who you were it seemed better to stop things before it got too complicated."

He looks down at his food while he chews slowly. "I get it now. I was pissed at first, I can't deny it. But now that I know who you are, I get it."

His understanding feels like a giant weight lifted from my shoulders. I hadn't realized how much it bothered me that he thought I'd left him hanging for fun. Especially not after the things we'd talked about that night.

That kiss.

"It was the best date I've ever been on," I find myself admitting.

His expression softens. "Me too. Demon baby included. How is he, by the way? Still scaring the shit out of everyone you meet?"

I point toward my bedroom door. "He's hanging in my closet until I need to ride the metro again."

"Does he like Mexican food? Maybe we should save him some."

This crazy conversation is making me forget about everything that's been troubling me. My big appointment tomorrow, my sleepless night and my flaky parents. That's what I've missed the most about him. He's the only person who can just roll with my strangeness and he makes everything fun.

"I guess we should get started on planning these parties, huh?"

He pulls out his phone. "Tell me your ideas and I'll take notes."

"Okay. But I just have one question first. Are we really not getting strippers?"

He laughs. "Woman, don't tempt me. I would love to see my brother fight a guy in a sequined thong. But for the sake of keeping him out of jail, I think we should stick with something boring."

"Right."

12

Din

FOR THE NEXT HOUR, WE EAT AND THROW OUT IDEAS. We immediately rule out all the usual stuff like paintball (too messy for Andre), camping (too scary for Casey), or sailing on Andre's yacht (too predictable). Trying to come up with something that satisfies everyone seems impossible.

"This is harder than it should be. Maybe we'll just take them to Andre's penthouse and leave them there alone. That's probably what he really wants anyway."

I'm really not as bitter as I sound. Maybe just a little jealous that my brother found his perfect match while mine leaves me in restaurants and sends me fake dicks at work.

"Tempting. Well, I would love to at least decide on the date. I need to make sure I'm off shift that night."

"Off shift," I repeat, suddenly realizing I'm probably monopolizing her time after a long day.

"I'm a nurse," she reminds me.

"Believe me, I remember. You have no idea how tempting it was to get hit by another car."

She hides her face behind her hand but nothing can hide the blush climbing her neck. It's fascinating how such a breathtaking woman can be so uncomfortable getting a compliment.

"What made you want to be a nurse?"

When she hesitates, I nudge her shoulder. "Come on. I wasn't kidding when I said we should get to know each other better. After this, we'll be seeing each other occasionally. It shouldn't be awkward."

"I wanted to help people," she admits finally.

"That's very noble."

Clearly uncomfortable with the praise, she shrugs.

"It's a scary thing being sick. You're away from home and everything that's familiar. Sometimes a friendly face can make all the difference. I wanted to make a difference."

Something about the way she speaks makes me think she knows from experience. Was she sick as a child? The thought of her once being alone and helpless tightens my throat.

"I bet you bring a lot of happiness to everyone you treat. You hide it with that wild behavior but you care about people. You're the type to go the extra mile for your patients, to make being hurt just a little bit more bearable. And I bet they never forget you."

I lean forward until our noses are almost touching.

"I certainly didn't."

I get up for some water, giving her a little space. Ariana is like a skittish animal. If you corner her, she will bolt. Or bite your face off. So I turn the conversation to banal, everyday things. Before long she relaxes and finishes off the enchiladas.

She clearly loves Mexican, a fact I file away for future use.

After we're finished eating, I pack up the food and put the containers in her refrigerator.

"You put the food away? Without being asked."

I pause, unsure where she's going with this. "I did."

"Geez, if I was the swooning type I'd need a fainting couch right about now," she mutters.

As usual her commentary makes me smile. Every moment with her is unpredictable. She's just ... fun.

Then I grab a wet sponge and start wiping off the counters. When I'm done, I rinse the sponge out before putting it neatly back into the holder by the faucet. Ariana watches from her new spot on the couch.

"Wow. You brought dinner and you cleaned up after? Where have you been all my life?"

I give her a look.

"*Oh right*. I ghosted you. I'm such a bitch."

My shoulders are shaking with laughter as I wash my hands before drying them carefully on the tea towel hanging in front of the sink. I join her on the couch, sitting on the other end so I don't crowd her.

"We were raised wealthy. But our father came from humble means. He made sure we were true gentlemen. Although clearly Andre got most of that along with most of the talent."

"That's definitely not true."

"Maybe a little. Fortune smiles on some of us more than others."

She suddenly looks sad. "You don't have to tell me that. But fortune smiled on you, too. There's no way the Lavin brand would have gotten so big without your input also."

"Know a lot about business, huh?" I ask teasingly.

"I know a little something. My father owns one of the biggest investment firms in South America."

My eyebrows lift at this bit of unexpected news. "Yeah?"

"Yeah. Apparently he's kind of a big deal. That is, when he's not too busy feuding with my mom or trying to send me checks as a substitute for his attention."

"I'm sorry you had to deal with that. But I'm grateful they were together long enough to create you."

She smiles sheepishly. "The irony is the reason they hate each other is because they're exactly alike. They'll both do anything for money. I've always been the referee in the middle of their battles. It's gotten old, this year in particular."

"Someone once told me families are complicated."

"Using my own words against me. I deserved that. But immature as my father can be, he's a mastermind at business. He used to always say a smart man hires men who are smarter than he is."

"Sounds like good advice."

"I'm just saying, you have a different skill set from your brother. No offense to Andre, but he's not the most approachable person ever. You have this way of making every person you meet feel like a friend. I bet that comes in really handy doing your international whatever it was you said you did."

By the end of her speech, her eyes are fiery.

"You're the roommate," I blurt suddenly.

She looks confused.

"Last year, Andre thought he'd lost Casey for good. There was this tabloid thing... Anyway, he said her roommate yelled at him. That she told him he'd fucked up and then slammed the door on him."

She makes a face. "Guilty."

I crack up. "I should have known then it was you."

"Being a bitch is kind of my brand."

"You were being *protective*. It seems like you take care of a lot of people. Your friends. Your parents. Your patients. Who takes care of you?"

She picks at a loose thread on the corner of the couch. "You think you've got me all figured out."

"No, not even close. But I will get there."

"That's what I'm afraid of," she whispers.

A quick glance at my watch proves it's later than I thought.

"I should probably go so you can get back to whatever you were doing before."

"A whole lot of nothing."

When I look over, it seems like she's closer than she was before. She's curled her feet up on the couch and one of her toes is brushing the side of my leg. I grab her foot and tickle the bottom.

She shrieks with laughter. "No! I can't stand being tickled."

"That was just your subtle way of asking for a foot rub then?" My hands stop their feathery movements and start massaging instead.

Ariana sighs. When I look over a minute later, her eyes are closed. Then she moans.

I bite the inside of my cheek. It's torture listening to this while she's wiggling all over the couch next to me. She made those little sounds when I kissed her that night, too. Soft little whimpers and sweet little sighs that make a man imagine how she'll sound while he's inside her.

My hand inches up her leg, running over the smooth skin of her calf. I close my eyes. She's so damn soft.

Stop thinking about how soft she is.

Definitely don't think about how wet she is.

When I open my eyes, Ariana is watching me with a knowing little smile. She's on her back with both her legs stretched into my lap. While I watch, she lets her legs fall open. The shorts she has on are loose enough that I can see her black panties.

I groan and Ariana pushes her foot harder into my lap. I squeeze her ankle in warning. "You just can't resist starting trouble, can you?"

"That doesn't look like trouble."

"Doesn't it? Feels like it to me."

She bites her lip. "It looks like it would feel good."

I release her legs and climb across the couch until I'm nearly straddling her. She lets out a soft murmur as our bodies touch.

"Why can't I stay away from you? You really have cast a spell on me, haven't you?"

Her hand curls behind my neck and pulls me closer.

"I just want to know what it would have been like."

At my raised eyebrow, she continues. "That night, if your phone hadn't rang. If we'd left together. I just want to know..."

Our lips crash together as if on cue, neither of us able to wait a minute longer before giving in to this undeniable pull. Because we both know where things were going that night before we'd gotten interrupted.

To her bed.

Or my bed.

Or against the wall.

Kissing me seems to have given her permission to stop holding back. No longer coy, Ariana wraps her legs around my waist and is practically humping me from below. Her hips undulate and the loose fabric of her shorts is no match for how hard we're grinding. She gasps into my mouth as I rub against the right spot.

"*Oh my god*. That feels so good. Vin."

Hearing her calling out for me is like injecting liquid sex into my veins. My hands caress her legs before moving up to yank at the waistband of her shorts. I lift up only long enough to pull them off and throw them over my shoulder. The sight of her in simple black cotton panties should not be so insanely sexy. But this is Ariana and everything she does excites me.

Especially when her soft little hand cups me through my trousers.

"*Madre di Dio.*"

Her laughter somehow makes my dick swell even harder. She's so unpredictable that I can imagine her laughing like that even with my dick in her mouth. Of course that image doesn't help my situation at all. Just the mental image of her on her knees in front of me is almost enough to make me blow.

"We have to stop."

"What?" Ariana pants before grabbing the front of my shirt and pulling me down for another kiss.

This one goes even longer, until I have her pert little ass in my hands holding her in place while I roll my hips. She's so wet, I bet it's all over my pants. Her scent is all over me and I want it in my mouth. My tongue is on the way to heaven when I spy the box I brought with me. It reminds me that just a few days ago we were still in a place where she wanted to send me a box of exploding dicks.

Ariana isn't ready for what I want. To her, this is just a chance to get a little sex on the side since we didn't get there two years ago. She doesn't want to date me. Hell, some days she doesn't even seem to like me that much.

Getting in any deeper is only going to make things more unclear.

"Baby, we have to stop."

She moans and the sound tugs at my resolve. But I lean back and shake my head, trying to clear my brain of the mental image of licking her pussy.

I don't want just a taste of her. And if that's all she can offer, then it's best I go now.

"You don't want a relationship, do you?"

The words clear the lust from her eyes immediately. "What? No. Who said anything about a relationship?"

I stand and run my fingers through my hair. All the blood isn't flowing to my brain properly yet. But I have enough sense to walk to the kitchen and grab my suit jacket.

Ariana sits up looking disgruntled. "I thought we were just having fun."

"We are having fun. I always have fun with you. That's why I need to leave before it gets out of hand. Besides, I brought you something that can help you out."

I point to the box on the floor next to the couch. "Those will do you a lot more good than me."

With one last look at her sprawled on the couch, rumpled and sexy, I leave.

A second later, something crashes against the other side of the door I just closed, making me jump.

"Asshole!" she yells from inside.

I laugh. "Damn, those dildos are solid."

I've just stepped off the elevator at Andre's penthouse when I remember why it's a bad idea. Casey lives here now. He's about to get married.

He doesn't need his little brother showing up randomly with his problems.

I hit the button for the elevator again. I'll have to talk to him at work tomorrow. Just as the doors open, I hear Andre call my name.

"Philippe? *Cosa fai?* Why are you just standing in the hallway?"

"I was coming to talk to you. But then I remembered. I don't want to interrupt."

I'm rambling but he seems to get the point because he holds the door open wider.

"Get in here."

I walk in and slip my shoes off by the door. The place used to be all white, black and stainless steel. The ultimate bachelor pad. But now it looks lived in, like the kind of place you could put your feet up. Casey has a fondness for blankets and as usual there's a huge knit throw hanging off the white sectional. There's a stack of paperback books on the entry table. They look brand new.

Andre motions to the books. "Casey just brought them home. There's this independent bookstore she likes to visit each month. She calls it *stimulating the economy*." He looks down at the books affectionately.

"I didn't get it before."

Andre looks startled at the change of subject.

"Get it?"

"The thing with Casey. Last year, you were losing your mind when you couldn't find her. I didn't understand how you could be so far gone over someone you just met. I didn't get it then. I get it now."

He doesn't say anything just watches me. Like he's deconstructing all my parts, trying to find where I'm coming apart at the seams.

"Where is Casey, anyway?"

The place seems so quiet. I've gotten used to Casey's cheerful chatter whenever I come visit. She doesn't have any siblings so she's thrilled with her new role as honorary sister and fusses over me excessively. It annoys the hell out of Andre, so naturally I love it all the more.

"She's taking a bath. She won't be out for a while. She's doing a mud mask."

"Why do women do that shit?"

"It's good for your pores." Andre glances at me from the corner of his eye. "That's what I've heard."

"Never mind, I don't want to know why you know that." I can't stand still. I pace back and forth across the carpet.

"What's going on? Why are you sweating?"

"Because she makes me crazy!"

"Who? I didn't even know you were seeing someone."

"I can't tell you who it is. She doesn't want anyone to know." Not that Ariana has said that explicitly but it's pretty clear she's happy to keep our prior acquaintance under wraps.

"Okay. Casey will be disappointed. She's gotten the idea to play matchmaker for you. That's what the dinner invitation for this weekend was about."

I glare at him. "And you were going to let me be ambushed? Nice, brother. I'll let you explain to her why I can't make it."

He watches as I continue to pace. Inside, I'm a ball of restless energy. All the fury and passion that Ariana always stirs up is roiling inside like a kettle ready to blow.

"I just want to take care of her but anytime I try, it drives her away. I don't know what I'm doing."

"I'll let you in on a secret," Andre says. "None of us know what we're doing."

"*Papa* always knew."

"He was different."

"Tell me about it. What would he tell me to do?"

Andre thinks for a moment.

"To be what she needs. Tomorrow go over there and talk to her. Maybe she's lashing out at you because she doesn't know any other way to be."

"It hurts my pride to admit it but when I try to get serious, she runs the other way. But then there are times when she holds me like she'll never let go."

I feel ridiculous throwing out these feelings but one look at his face reassures me I'm not alone. My brother truly understands just how insane one woman can make you.

He considers my words for a moment before clapping a reassuring hand on my shoulder.

"You and I, we learned from the best but some people don't know how to love. If she's the one, *teach her*. Love isn't just words. It's action. Be the man she needs you to be."

13

Ariana

THE NEXT MORNING, I'M UP BEFORE THE ALARM GOES off. After a night of tossing and turning, there's no point in pretending I can sleep anymore. With my erratic schedule insomnia is a constant friend but I wouldn't have been able to sleep last night anyway.

I have to see my oncologist today. It's the big one. The five-year follow-up appointment.

My mom never called me back last night. Maybe she had to get a later flight. I call her again but it goes straight to voicemail.

"Where are you, Mom?"

Maybe she got in really late and is still asleep. If there's one thing Ingrid Larsson takes seriously, it's beauty sleep.

I spend a little time scrolling on Instagram, looking at beautiful pictures of kitchen renovations and girls sharing coupon codes for various boutiques.

It's perfectly mindless and exactly what I need right now. Anything to take my mind off the milestone today represents. Five years is a significant number for a lot of cancer survivors. As my oncologist likes to tell me, it doesn't mean I'm "cured" but my chance of reoccurrence goes way down. I won't have to come in to see her as often anymore.

For me, this appointment represents being able to live without feeling like I'm holding my breath the whole time.

I take a quick shower and then put on some comfy leggings and a long shirt. My appointments are usually scheduled for the morning just in case she wants to do any imaging. You can't eat or drink anything before most of those tests. So I've gotten used to skipping breakfast on these days.

My phone still shows no unread emails, no calls and no new texts. I rub my face before calling my mom again. Maybe she's in the shower right now and hasn't seen my other calls. She knows what a big deal this is.

It goes straight to voicemail.

Pushing aside the disappointment, I grab my purse and stuff a water bottle in there since I'm usually thirsty afterward.

My car is parked two blocks away since parking in Adam's Morgan is always terrible. A few years ago Dr. Rose moved her practice to the neighboring state of Virginia. It's a bit of a drive but I don't mind the trip. If there's a chance that I might get bad news, I don't want it from a stranger.

The traffic is relatively light since it's a weekday and before long I'm cruising down I-95 with the windows down. It's a nice day and that feels like an omen. I latch onto the feeling with everything I have. Today has to be good news.

The doctor's office is in a large building that's connected to a hospital. I see the sign first. *Northern Virginia Oncology Partners.*

It always amazes me when I come out to the suburbs and remember that I don't have to fight for a parking space. I park right across from the front door under a tree bursting with vibrant pink flowers. I glance at the clock on the dash.

It's almost time.

I call my mom again. When it goes to voicemail, I don't bother leaving a message. Tears prick my eyes.

This is why you don't get your hopes up, Ari. People disappoint you.

This time I thought she might actually come through for me. That she would show up when it was important. But I don't have time for this. I can't be late.

I grab my bag and lock the car behind me. As I approach the front door, I'm mentally preparing myself for what's about to happen. The exam and blood work isn't so bad. For me, the hardest part of coming here every few months is the awful sense of dread that haunts me for a week afterward until I get the all clear. Waiting to hear if you're okay is excruciating and it hasn't gotten much easier over the years. I just thought, this once, maybe I wouldn't have to do it alone.

Once I reach the door, I suddenly can't do it.

I put a hand to my throat and close my eyes. My breath is coming fast and hard. There's a wooden bench to the left of the door so I walk to it and sink down gratefully. I keep my head tipped down so no one will see me crying.

Someone sits next to me and I look up, startled. Vin doesn't look at me, keeping his eyes on something in the distance.

"How did you find me?"

"Maybe I have radar for when you need me."

"Radar, huh? The kind that leads you to my exact location in another state?"

"Mmm, hmm."

I swipe at the tears on my cheeks with the edge of my sleeve, wishing that for once I'd remembered to pack practical things in my purse instead of just lip gloss and junk food.

He finally glances at me from the corner of his eye. "Or maybe I'm a stalker who followed you from your apartment."

My laughter is muffled by the edge of my sleeve. "There he is. There's the Vin I know and–"

I cough, shocked at what I almost said.

"You're here for you?" he asks quietly.

I know what he means. Technically I could be here in a professional capacity, maybe applying for a new job since I'm a nurse. But I'm pretty sure he already knows what's up thanks to my little emotional breakdown so I just nod.

"Then I'm here for you, too."

After signing in at the reception desk, I take the clipboard filled with forms the office seems to need signed every time I come here.

Vin sits next to me. As usual he's dressed in a designer suit and looks completely out of place in regular life, like a prince amongst commoners. Especially right next to my leggings and T-shirt. His foot taps a steady rhythm on the carpet, scratching the rough fibers.

Tap.

Tap.

Tap.

His features are tight, the line between his eyes more prominent.

I know that intense look. He's worried about me. The lump that's been in my stomach loosens a little bit. I still can't believe he's here. He arrived just in the nick of time, knight in shining armor style.

"This is actually one of the hardest parts."

His foot stops moving. "What?"

I motion around the room. "The waiting part. Sitting here with nothing to do but think about potential bad outcomes."

He grabs my hand and his thumb moves back and forth over my knuckle.

"Tell me what to do. I don't know what to do. I want to do the right thing."

Hearing him so unsure actually warms my heart. I squeeze his hand back.

"You are doing the right thing. You're here."

He lets out a shaky breath. "Good. Because I have never felt so helpless in my life."

We sit in silence while I initial the forms in various places. Then after I give all the information back to the nurse at the desk, I take my seat. There are a few other people waiting, an elderly couple sitting in the corner, a guy who looks about my age and even a pregnant woman. I take a deep breath.

God, cancer really is a bitch.

"Tell me something," I whisper.

His presence has calmed me a lot but I can feel the panic hovering just beneath the surface. At any moment, they're going to call my name and I'm going to have to go back there alone. This is as far as Vin can go. I'm not ready for him to see me in a medical gown.

Just no. I wish I didn't have to see it either.

"Like what," he whispers back, way too loudly.

"Anything. I just need to take my mind off what's about to happen."

"Okay. Um... I told my assistant that box of dicks you sent was a modern art display from Europe."

What the hell? I turn to look at him. So does the pregnant woman who is close enough to overhear. My lips clamp together to hold in a giggle.

"Okay that definitely worked."

"Now you tell me something," he whispers, still loud as hell.

I lean over and kiss his cheek, drawing in the scent of Vin and comfort. Hopefully it'll be enough to keep me going.

"I'm glad you're such a stalker."

His eyes shine. "Anytime, baby."

"Ariana Silva?" A nurse wearing pink scrubs looks around the room expectantly.

"That's my cue." I grab my purse.

When Vin starts to stand up, I put a hand on his arm.

"Could you wait for me? Actually, it's probably going to take a long time. I mean, you can leave really. I'm okay now."

He shakes his head. "I'll be right here waiting for you when you come out."

"Are you sure?" I feel kind of bad that he'll be sitting here in this depressing waiting room with nothing but expired magazines to keep him company.

But that look is back in his eyes again, the one that says he's not going to back down.

"What did I tell you outside? When you need me, I'm here."

14

Din

THE WAITING ROOM IS QUIET. I SIT IN A RIGID CHAIR next to a stack of magazines with my eyes glued to the door that just closed behind Ariana.

On the outside, I'm the picture of calm. That's what she needed from me so that's what I managed to give her. Inside is another story.

It was unsettling to see this new side of her. This soft-spoken, unsure, scared version of Ariana. It physically hurt to see my beautiful girl sitting on that bench looking so defeated. If I could I would slay dragons to protect her.

But I can't save her from this.

Everything makes sense now. All of it. The crazy shit she does to push me away. The longing I see in her eyes while she watches her friends with their partners. She doesn't think she'll get to have that because she won't be here long enough.

And she might be right.

I run a hand over my face.

My emotions do not get to take center stage right now. This is not about me. This is about the woman who doesn't even know she has my heart wrapped around her little finger.

This is about the bone-deep fear gnawing away at my gut that fate brought me back into her life too late.

She has cancer.

I'm falling in love with her and she has cancer.

The time that elapses between her name being called and when she eventually comes back seems like an eternity. Really, it's probably only two hours. But I don't move my ass from that seat any longer than it takes to stand and stretch my legs every half hour or so. If Ariana needs me for anything I plan to be right here.

Finally the door opens and she emerges. At least her eyes aren't red anymore and she seems in better spirits as she waves at the nurse behind the front desk.

She motions for me to follow her. "I'm ready."

When we emerge into the afternoon sun, it almost seems incongruous to hear birds chirping and see lazy white clouds moving across the blue sky.

The contrast between the somber office and the vibrant life outside its walls only makes the former seem even more dismal.

If I hadn't seen her leaving this morning, I would have never known she was here. I send up a prayer to *Papa* for putting me in the right place at the right time. Then another for Mitch, the cabbie who'd been more than happy to drive like a maniac to keep up with her in exchange for an extra five hundred dollars.

We stop next to her car. The tree she parked under provides some shade but has littered the top of her vehicle with flower petals.

She fiddles with the strap of her purse nervously. "You probably have a million questions."

"No questions. This isn't the time. Is there anywhere else you need to go?"

"This is it. I don't ever plan anything else when I have these appointments. Afterward, I just want to go home."

"Then let's go home." I pause before reaching for the passenger side door of her car. "I guess I do have a question. Will you give me a ride?"

She looks around the parking lot. "How did you get here?"

"It involves a cab driver who was happy to play James Bond and all the cash I had in my wallet."

And every dollar was worth it to see her smile.

Back at her apartment, I can feel Ariana watching me. Probably waiting for me to start asking questions. Or waiting to see if I make an excuse to leave.

Instead I do what I've always done. Make myself at home.

"I'll make us some tea. That seems to be the thing when you need to relax. You can get comfortable on the couch." I take off my suit jacket and hang it over a bar stool. Then I roll up the sleeves of my dress shirt so they don't get in my way.

She drops her bag by the kitchen island.

"Don't you have to go back to work? Won't people wonder where you are?"

I shake my head. "I already told Andre that I would be out for the day."

"He didn't ask why?"

"I told him my girl was sick. He understands."

"Your girl?" she challenges, her eyes on mine.

I hold her gaze wanting to make sure she knows just how serious I am. "My girl. My one and only."

No response to that.

She watches silently while I unearth an electric kettle from one of her cabinets and put the water on to boil. Normally we don't have to fill every second with chatter, one of the things I love about spending time with her. But this time the silence is awkward.

So awkward.

"You're making me nervous just watching me like that. Is this the part where you kick me out?"

She shakes her head. "Are you really going to pretend everything is okay?"

"I know it's not okay. But you've had a rough morning. So have I."

"You just found out I had cancer."

"Had?"

"Yes. I'm in remission."

All at once my muscles relax and I feel like I can breathe again. The overwhelming sense of relief is so powerful my legs almost give out and I have to grab on to the counter so I don't fall.

She's in remission.

I don't fool myself that things are fine now. But after spending the last few hours convinced fate had betrayed me, I am grasping on to every last bit of hope like a lifeline.

Knowing too much emotion will scare her off, I take a second to pull myself together. Then I think *fuck it* and come around the counter. I lift her straight into my arms.

"Ari." It's all I can get out. Just her name before my throat closes again.

She's rigid in my arms at first, her entire upper body as straight as a ruler. Then she melts into the embrace, wrapping her legs around my waist. When her fingers curl into the hair at the nape of my neck, I feel it all the way down to my toes. Her touch electrifies me.

"Vin. Shhh now. It's okay." She strokes my hair while whispering more nonsense words.

"I just spent the last few hours thinking it was too late for us. That I'd lost you before I even had you."

I can't lose this. I can't lose *her*.

"I really am okay. Vin? Did you hear me?"

She pushes back slightly so she can see my face. I'm not ashamed of the moisture on my cheeks. Her thumbs brush it away before she leans her forehead against mine.

"This was my five year scan. The big one. After this, I'm considered to be out of the danger zone. As much as any survivor can be, anyway."

"It can come back after that?"

There's resignation in her eyes. "It can always come back."

I'd give anything to take this for her, to keep her safe from the faceless threat that she's lived under for years. But all I can do is be here for her. To take care of her the way she takes care of everyone else.

"That's enough talk for now. Do you want a foot massage? Or a nap?"

She slaps my chest lightly.

"Ow. What was that for?"

"We need to talk about this. We can't pretend it doesn't matter."

Unable to resist any longer, I capture her mouth. Her lips soften beneath mine, all the tension in her body flowing into the kiss.

"Everything about you matters. But I don't need to ask questions when my girl is tired and still has that haunted look in her eyes. None of the answers will change the fact that I'm exactly where I'm supposed to be."

"I guess you know all my secrets now."

Thinking of all the strange things she's said and done to me since we met, I doubt I'll ever know all her secrets. But at least I'll have the time to discover some of them.

And I'll never be bored.

The whistle of the tea kettle startles us both. We laugh before I set her gently on her feet.

"I'll get the tea."

She nods. "I'll change into my pajamas. That's usually what I do after a morning of feeling like a lab rat."

I move the kettle off the heat to quiet the noise and then rummage through the cabinets until I find teabags. When I turn, Ari is still hovering at the edge of the kitchen with a tender, unsure look on her face.

"What is it, baby?"

She doesn't even make a face at the endearment.

"What if it's back? The cancer, I mean. Sure you don't want to bail?"

"If it's back then we'll deal with that. As far as me bailing," I walk over and tap her nose affectionately. "Just *try* and get rid of me."

15

Ariana

EVEN THOUGH I'M NOT CONVINCED BY HIS *WE DON'T need to talk about it* stance, I'm too tired to argue. Having tests done always leaves me feeling a little gloomy and violated. Through my own research I know it's actually common for cancer patients to develop PTSD from repeated screenings, every single new test making them feel the anxiety of a potential relapse all over again.

It's funny how I know all this stuff intellectually but it hits you in a different way when it's happening to you. So I go to my room to change. I decide to take a quick shower before I change into my oldest, comfiest nightshirt. It's long enough to reach my knees and I definitely don't feel compelled to wear pants around Vin. No doubt he'll be all in favor of us both going without.

When I come back out there's a steaming cup of tea waiting for me.

"Thank you. This is exactly what I needed."

Vin waves me over to the couch and I settle in next to him, snuggling right under his arm. The events of the morning and the prior sleepless night finally catch up to me. When I wake up, Vin smiles sheepishly.

"Sorry. I was trying not to move and wake you up."

"It's okay. Napping during the day is only going to mess up my sleep schedule anyway." I sit up, stretching out the ache in my back from being cramped in the same position. The television is on and there's an action movie playing.

And Oreo is asleep at his feet.

My eyes shoot to his in surprise.

"I guess she decided if her mama could trust me, she could too," he murmurs.

My phone rings from the kitchen pulling my attention from this minor miracle. It's still in my bag where I dropped it earlier. It stops ringing before I can reach it. I swipe to see who it was.

Missed call: DRAMA MAMA

With a sigh, I drop the phone back in my purse.

Vin looks up when I come back to the couch.

"It was my mom. Probably excuses about why she couldn't come today. Or more stories about the latest thing my father has done to get on her nerves."

He grabs my hand. "You don't owe anyone your attention today. Today is for you."

Somehow it's the exact right thing to say. No one would accuse me of being a martyr but I do have a bad habit of trying to make other people comfortable.

My patients at the hospital.

My parents.

My friends.

This is great at work but not so much at home. Maybe it's okay to spend a little time thinking about what I need. Vin was right that first night we met. I do push people away. But that's because it seems easier to be alone than deal with being disappointed in people all the time.

"You're right. I can deal with her tomorrow."

"Today, we do what you want to do."

"Anything I want?"

"Of course."

I swing a leg over his and straddle him. Vin groans and tries to hold my hips away from him.

"Ari, baby. What are you doing?"

"You said we could do anything I want."

"You want to do *that*? Now?"

His befuddlement is really cute. Not only that I could be interested in sex randomly but that I'd initiate it out of the blue. Who does he think he's dealing with?

I appreciate him taking care of me since I definitely needed a shoulder to lean on earlier. But I don't need anyone treating me like glass. I'm not fragile. I'm a frickin' boss.

And as I told my friends, I'm also really horny.

Don't judge me.

I roll my hips, gratified at the strangled groan that falls from his lips.

"What you said earlier, about giving me what I need? Did you mean it?"

His hands tighten on my hips, so hard I'm sure I'll have bruises in the shape of his fingers later. I love the pain, it makes me feel alive. Like I'm still here and can do some damage in this world.

"I love you. I would give you the beating heart from my chest if you'd let me."

My head falls forward and our lips meet, a furious class of lips and teeth. I am humbled by the things he says, completely and utterly undone. I don't know what I did to deserve this kind of love but for once I'm going to be selfish and take it.

"You could break my heart. I don't think I could bear it."

He stands with me in his arms and the blatant display of strength is sexy as hell.

"I never would. One day you'll believe it."

I point down the hall so he knows where my room is and he carries me the whole way, stumbling into the wall when I bite his neck.

"Woman, that mouth is going to get you into trouble."

"*Mmm*, trouble. You know how much I love that."

Together we crash on top of the bed, knocking a box of tissues and a paperback book off the nightstand. We're kissing like we can't breathe when we're apart and it's a struggle to get our clothes off with our mouths fused together. His shirt is probably in tatters with the way he ripped it off and my nightshirt doesn't fare much better. As soon as my shirt is gone, Vin's mouth trails over my chest. He pauses to kick off his pants, leaving him in black boxer briefs.

When he goes to take my bra off, my hand clasps his.

"What is it, baby?"

My mouth is suddenly dry as dust.

"Um, I have a scar. From a lumpectomy."

Showing my scar makes me feel more exposed than the loss of my clothes. Usually I keep my bra on in bed because it makes me more comfortable to keep it covered. But here, with Vin, for the first time I feel I can be truly naked.

He kisses me gently and waits to see what I'll do. I reach underneath and unhook my bra before sliding it off. His eyes land on the scar that runs down the side of my right breast like a red smile. Then he bows his head and places a gentle kiss there, like he's soothing it. Soothing me.

He lavishes the left breast with the same attention before his tongue trails down my stomach. My hips move with him, eagerly anticipating the moment his lips will reach the place that aches for him. When his mouth finally, *finally*, covers my pussy my hips buck up off the bed, the pleasure too sharp to hold still.

"Ariana. My beautiful little devil. You even taste like trouble."

My hands slide into his hair as his tongue rolls over my folds, playing with me like a piece of candy he doesn't want to eat too fast. Back and forth, every lick taking me closer and closer to heaven. My thighs shake but he doesn't let up until I'm screaming his name and gasping for breath.

He looks a little too satisfied with himself so when he leans back, I follow. Carefully, I slide onto the floor, on my knees next to him. He groans when I hook my fingers in the sides of his boxer briefs, tugging gently. He's so hard that he pops out immediately and I lick the tip, circling the head gently.

"Ariana, I'm too worked up. I don't think I can take this."

Ignoring him, I fist his entire length with a tight grip while lavishing the head with soft suctioning kisses. As his breath comes harder, I take him deeper, staring into his eyes as he bumps the back of my throat.

It's a challenge to take him that far but the look on his face makes it worth the effort. He groans and his fingers clench the sheets beside us, flexing with every pull of my mouth.

"*Ari?*"

His hands are in my hair now, trying to pull me away. But instead, I use my hand to stroke him softly before going back in to deep throat again.

"Oh god." He chants it now, a steady rhythm of words before it switches to Italian and I don't understand anymore.

Seeing him like this, completely at my mercy ratchets my own arousal higher. Especially when he opens his eyes again and our eyes connect while I'm taking him so deep.

"Fuck. I have to–"

At his anguished rasp, I stop immediately, chuckling when he groans. I need him inside me. I need to hold him closer.

He seems to sense my desperation because he leans over the bed to find his wallet.

"If I don't have a condom I'm going to cry," he jokes.

I lean over and pull open the nightstand. "There's a box in here."

He grabs it. I watch as he rips open the box and pulls out a strip of protection. With some guys the condom thing is awkward and I usually find a reason not to look. But not with Vin. His dark eyes stay on mine as he rolls on a condom, stroking himself the whole way.

My cheeks heat. Trust Vin to make putting on a condom a show.

When he climbs back in bed, I let out a sigh of satisfaction at the first touch of our naked bodies. Our skin sliding together feels so good.

His groan tells me he feels the same.

"Tell me what you want, my little devil."

Gentle suctioning kisses cover my throat in between his words. All while his hips move with a slow, grinding rhythm.

"You. Inside me."

His hand moves down to test my readiness and his sharp intake of breath tells me he loves what he finds. One finger curls deep, rubbing until I gasp his name. Then he grabs my thigh and wraps it around his waist.

I cry out when he thrusts deep, sliding right where I need him. My hips move with his like we've done this before a million times. With him, it's natural. I don't feel like I have to act sexy or do anything to make it good.

It's good because it's us.

It's great because I love him.

"Vin. *Please.*"

My pussy clenches and his hands tighten under my bottom. The unexpected caress there throws my orgasm into overdrive. I can barely hang on as I splinter apart, screaming his name.

"Ari. My sweet girl." His words devolve into a jumble of Italian until he pauses, his hips jerking in short, sharp thrusts like his pleasure is being pulled out of him.

The aftermath feels like we just survived a shipwreck. It takes a minute for my breathing to slow and for the ringing in my ears to subside.

But despite just screaming my head off, for the first time in ages, my soul feels calm.

While Vin takes a shower, I curl up in my bed completely content. Maybe it's just the aftereffect of great sex but I'm feeling uncharacteristically emotional.

He said some pretty heavy things to me today. That he wanted to be here when I needed him. That he would give me his beating heart.

I'm not the kind of girl who needs flowery words or all that romantic bullshit but I would have to be made of ice not to be affected by him. Vin doesn't pull any punches when he wants something. A fact that I admire while it also scares the hell out of me.

He's decided I'm what he wants and the pressure to be worthy of that is immense. This man deserves every good thing.

I am still not sure that I am going to be good for him.

"This is starting to get a little rough on my ego. You seem to spend so much time around me falling asleep."

At his words, I roll over to face him. His spectacular chest is on full display and all he's wearing is a towel around his waist. I pulled on my nightshirt but the way his eyes roam my body makes me feel like I shouldn't have bothered.

"I'm awake. Just thinking about everything."

He pulls on his boxer briefs, then turns in a circle until he notices his pants on the other side of the room. "I'd hoped to take your mind off all that."

I blatantly ogle his butt as he bends over and steps into his trousers. The man truly has a fine ass.

"You definitely did. I wouldn't mind if you did it again."

His fingers continue moving, buttoning up his shirt but his knowing eyes watch me as I struggle for words.

"I'm just saying, you could... stay. You don't have to rush off."

He leans down and brushes my hair off my forehead. "You aren't ready for that, baby."

When I go to protest, he kisses me.

"The first night I stay with you, I want it to be because you really want me here for good. Not because I just blew your mind in bed. I know I'm the best but that's no basis for a relationship."

It takes me a minute but when what he said sinks in, I hit him with a pillow.

"Blew *my* mind? Mister, I just blew *your* mind." I whack him with the pillow again. "And your dick. Don't forget that."

He collapses on top of me, laughing uncontrollably. "I won't be forgetting that anytime soon. Or ever. The sight of you looking up at me... *Dio,* now I'm getting hard again."

Satisfied, I sit back. "My work here is done."

"Ah, you really are evil woman. But I like you that way."

My hand twists in the front of his shirt to stop him when he goes to turn away. "Don't let this go to your head or anything but I'm really glad you were there today."

"Me too."

After a long, deep kiss that makes me want to yank him down for another round, he says goodbye and leaves, closing my bedroom door partially behind him. When I hear him start talking, I lean forward to hear. I can barely make out the words but it's enough for me to realize he's saying goodbye to the dog. My heart melts into a puddle of goo.

What am I going to do with this guy?

A few seconds later, the front door closes. I lean back into the pillows with a sigh. After a few minutes Oreo scratches at my partially open bedroom door until there's enough room for her to come in. She hops up on the bed to curl at my feet.

"We like him, huh? He's handsome and kind and has an ass that won't quit. But I can't get too deep with him yet. Not until I get my results back."

Oreo gives a quick bark of agreement. Then she rolls over and splays her legs wide open.

"Yeah, tell me about it. He has the same effect on me."

Grabbing another pillow, I shove it under my head trying to find a comfortable angle. I'm hit with a sudden wave of exhaustion. As I fall asleep, I can't stop thinking that fatigue is one of the earliest signs of cancer.

16

Din

THE MORNING OF MY BROTHER'S WEDDING DAWNS crisp and clear. I decide to bring Ari breakfast since it's a good excuse to come over early. Since we can't go to the wedding together, I have to make sure I get my Ariana fix beforehand.

Ariana leaves the apartment first, patting my cheek when I ask why.

"Women need more time to get ready for these things," she says before kissing me softly. "All you guys do is comb your hair and stuff your junk in a tuxedo."

"You don't know my brother very well," I reply.

But when I arrive at the Fitz-Harrington, I discover I don't know my brother as well as I thought I did either.

My brother, usually the picture of elegance, is on the phone every few minutes nervously checking some detail or other. Normally I would tease him but I can't when I notice his hands shaking as he picks up the phone *again* to ask the wedding planner if Casey needs anything.

I even let him fuss over my suit since it's a new design. He insisted on making our tuxedos entirely on his own, using none of his junior designers. So I stand still as he checks each stitch and every button. If this calms his nerves, then I'll stand here like a mannequin as long as he needs.

Until he comes at me with a tube of something that looks suspiciously like the mascara Ariana wears everyday.

"*What is that?* Don't put that crap on my face."

Andre sighs. "It's for your eyebrows. It keeps them in place."

"My eyebrows are already in place. They're on my face, exactly as they should be."

Andre hands the small tube to the blond man hovering at his side, who glares at me before putting it back in his massive case. He's been tormenting us both with a wide array of creams and powders from his vault of horrors.

"I've already got powder on my face. What other indignities must I suffer?" I mutter in Italian.

"The things you do for your family. I'm just glad you seem better," Andre comments, his dark eyes scanning over me like he's looking for flaws.

"I am. Your advice was spot on."

He smiles. "Good. Thank you for everything you've done to make this day happen. I know I made your life more difficult with the bachelor party thing."

"You made my life impossible with that shit. But we got it done."

Our joint bachelor and bachelorette party had turned out to be something the gossip magazines would be talking about for ages. Instead of doing something cliché, we'd ended up hosting an elegant *Cirque du Soleil* themed party two days ago instead. Small and intimate, the dancers moved through the crowd performing right along-side the party attendees. While they hadn't exactly been scantily clad, their strong, lithe bodies were somehow sexier than any stripper I've ever seen.

"How did you come up with the idea to hire those dancers? It was elegant but sensual. Casey loved it."

"Ariana came up with the idea actually. She said if she couldn't have Magic Mike then at least she could look at muscular men in tights."

He bursts into laughter. "Of course. That woman is insane. But Casey loves her. And she did help us get back together even though she didn't mean to. She meant it when she told me to fuck off. She *really* meant it," he mumbles under his breath.

I struggle to wipe the smile off my face. My brother still has no idea that insane woman is the love of my life.

This last week we've existed in a bubble outside of time. I've spent each evening at her place, bringing her takeout from all my favorite places in the city.

We talk.

We laugh.

We make love.

But we don't talk of the future or the test results, which still haven't come back. Ariana admitted they usually don't take this long and I could hear the worry she refuses to voice.

A waiter knocks once on the open door before wheeling in a tray of champagne.

"Delivery! Man, I love working here. There's always something bonkers going on."

Andre's head lifts. "Bonkers?"

The waiter chuckles to himself as he uncorks one of the bottles. "Yeah, I just saw some chick in a white dress running down the halls. Can you say runaway bride?"

Andre pales.

I snatch the champagne bottle out of the waiter's hand. "This is the groom."

The waiter looks over at Andre nervously. "Oh. Sorry about your old lady. Maybe she's coming back."

"Go." I point to the door and he scurries out without another word.

"Philippe? I need you to do something for me."

"Anything, brother."

"Casey. Find her. Make sure." He leans over and puts his hands on his knees.

I lead him to a chair and help him sit.

"That guy saw a random woman running. It doesn't mean it's Casey. But I'll go check."

As soon as I'm out of his sight, I'm practically running down to the other Presidential Suite where Casey is getting ready. I knock on the door rapidly. Ariana answers it and then immediately moves forward so no one inside can see me.

"Mr. Lavin! What can I do for you?" Her words are professional but her eyes are eating me up.

Ariana isn't ready for our friends to know about us. I understand and I respect that. This is a new step for her, being serious with someone. The fact that I'm about to be related through marriage to one of her best friends makes this a sensitive thing.

"Is Casey in there?"

"Yeah, she's just getting the finishing touches on her makeup."

I let out a long breath. "Good. Someone saw a woman wearing a white dress running through the hotel. Andre's freaking out thinking it was her."

Ariana laughs. "Actually that was someone Casey knew from high school. That bitch showed up in her old wedding dress and I told her to take her ass home."

"That's ridiculous but also really funny."

"Maybe not so funny in the moment. Casey was pretty upset at first. But I handled it."

"Yes, you did. I really want to kiss you right now," I whisper.

"Save a dance for me later, Mr. Lavin." With a wink, she shuts the door.

The good news is I get to tell my brother he does not have a runaway bride.

The bad news is I have to get through this entire wedding standing across from the woman I love, while pretending we barely know each other.

After that the wedding went off without a hitch. The reception has been smooth sailing, minus a few minor hiccups, and I'm counting the minutes until I can ask Ariana to dance without making anyone suspicious.

She winks at me from her place by the bar. The peach color of her gown brings out the honey tones in her hair and the plunging neckline has attracted the attention of every man she walks by. Including the one currently standing next to her looking like he wants to bury his face in the soft mounds.

I grit my teeth. That's it. I'm going over there.

As if she can hear me, Ari sets her glass of champagne down on the bar and saunters over. I meet her halfway and we blend into the crowd of people already dancing.

"What's this I hear about you playing Superman?"

"What?"

"You saved someone from choking?"

"It was nothing. One of Casey's friends ate too much cake. I slapped her on the back. That was it."

Ariana purses her lips. "The brunette with the bob?"

"Yeah. I think so."

Her fingers tighten on my shoulder as we continue to move across the dance floor. "The one Casey wanted to set you up with?"

This feels like dangerous territory.

"I don't remember. You look beautiful by the way."

She laughs. "You really are a charmer. I have to get out of here before they do that stupid bouquet toss. But come find me in the bar downstairs after that."

"I *really* wish I could kiss you right now."

A half an hour later, I come back into the ballroom. Right as they announced the bouquet toss, I got an urgent work email and went outside to handle it.

Like she has radar, *Mamma* appears as soon as I'm sneaking back in. She wrinkles her nose at the sight of the phone in my hand.

"Really, Philippe? It's your brother's wedding. You're supposed to be having fun. In fact, there's a very nice girl I could introduce you to."

"I can't, *Mamma*. I have to handle all the work stuff so that Andre doesn't have to. It's his day."

She pauses as if she can sense I'm not being completely truthful but isn't sure how to prove it.

I kiss her cheek, sensing my window to escape her trap is closing. "I have to go. I see the head of our marketing agency. I have to network."

I've met James Lawson multiple times but I'm not sure if he'll recognize me on sight. He doesn't look all that happy to be here, actually. He's staring glumly at the dance floor.

Mamma appears at the edge of my vision. I sigh. I'm going to have to look busy or I'll never escape her matchmaking. So I stop next to James and lean over.

"You're supposed to at least pretend to be happy at these things," I comment conspiratorially.

He glances over with a blank look.

I hold out a hand. "Philippe Lavin. I'm not sure if you remember me. I'm the brother of that sickeningly happy guy on the dance floor."

"I remember. You've been to the agency a few times for meetings. James Lawson."

I incline my head toward Andre and Casey who are currently kissing like they're about to tear each other's clothes off.

"They're ridiculously happy."

"Yes, they are." He grimaces. Then he seems to catch himself, pasting a smile on his face. "Marriage isn't for me but I wish them nothing but the best."

"It's funny, I used to feel the same way. But lately I've been thinking it might be nice to have someone to come home to. Someone who is happy to see me."

It's stupid confessing all this to a stranger but since we don't know each other, it seems safer somehow.

James tugs at the collar of his shirt, his face turning red.

"I thought that once, but take it from me buddy. If you want someone who is happy to see you when you come home, get a dog. It's cheaper."

He takes a final gulp of his champagne before placing the glass on the tray of a passing waiter.

Well, okay then. It seems I'm not the only one having problems in the romance department. But at least I'm trying. Since I can't tell anyone about Ariana, I'm forced to navigate these new and confusing feelings on my own.

And I definitely can't talk about them with her. She's totally on board with taking our relationship to the next physical level but she's still keeping a barbed wire fence around her heart, no matter how often I tell her I love her.

I can see in her eyes that she wants to say it back.

My beautiful little devil thinks I don't understand but I do. She's scared to let go until she finally gets the word from her doctor that she's fine. Those test results are like a bulletproof window between us.

I'm worried as well. She told me it usually doesn't take this long to get the results, unless there's some sort of backlog.

It usually doesn't take this long.

I close my eyes, amazed at my own stupidity. She's gotten the test results back, of course she has.

But would she tell me that right before my brother's wedding? No. She's used to dealing with things on her own and she wouldn't want to pull my focus from my family before such an important event. Because that's what my girl does. She puts everyone else's needs above her own and I've been oblivious enough this week to allow it to happen.

A cold spike rams through my heart.

She didn't tell me, which can only mean one thing.

17

Ariana

I REALLY HAVE TO STOP HANGING IN BARS.

The bartender hands me a glass of club soda and I take a small sip. Casey is upstairs dancing the night away with her new husband. Vin got to watch his beloved brother get married with no distractions.

I did it. I got through it.

Now I feel like crying.

I put my phone to my ear and listen to the voicemail I got from Dr. Rose two days ago again. Every time I play it, part of me hopes I'll hear something different. Something other than *abnormal* and *more testing*.

All the ways she avoided saying what we both know to be true.

It's back.

In a moment of petulance, I forward the message from Dr. Rose to my mother. I doubt she'll even listen to it. If it doesn't come attached to a check from my father, I doubt she'll care.

As I sit at the bar and drink my club soda, all I can think of is what's about to happen. The thought of replaying the last few years over again makes me want to cry. Is this what I can look forward to for the rest of my life, a constant rotation of testing and worry? Never feeling safe to get invested in anything and getting pieces of my body cut out every few years?

Worse, this time I'll be dragging Vin along for the ride. He loves me so much. If it was just me, I could take it. I'm a survivor. It's what I do. But he has no idea the toll this process can take on a person and their loved ones. His heart is in my hands and I'm going to trample it by dying on him.

I honestly have never felt worse.

After a few minutes, I look over and notice the woman sitting on my left. Brunette. Blue eyes. Panicked expression.

"*Fucking hell.*" I point at her with the same hand holding my drink. "If you're down here..."

Anya bursts into laughter that sounds suspiciously like crying. "You're the maid of honor!"

Her words make my shoulders slump. I am the maid of honor and I'm hiding out instead of celebrating with one of my best friends. Poor Casey is probably wondering where the hell her bridal party has gone.

I bang my forehead against the bar top. "We are terrible friends. You know that, right?"

"I'm willing to concede the possibility. To be fair, I almost got killed by a cupcake just now, so I'm probably not making the best decisions."

The bartender sets a drink down in front of her on one of those fancy white napkins. Anya hands him her credit card.

"Well, at least I don't feel quite as bad now." I raise my glass in a toast. "To the last ones standing."

"The last ones," she echoes. Her face crumples.

Uh oh. I know why I'm drinking alone at the bar in the middle of my friend's wedding reception. But clearly Anya is having some kind of crisis, too.

I wave to the bartender. "I have a feeling we're going to need more drinks."

We sit in silence for a while, each of us lost in our own thoughts. I wish I could have a real drink but I've already had some champagne tonight. I cut back on alcohol when I was first diagnosed. My body has been stressed enough so I don't need to add liver damage to the mix.

"So, what's your deal?"

Anya's voice slurs slightly and I make a note to slow down with the drinks. She hasn't noticed I'm drinking club soda yet so she probably thinks we're getting drunk together. I signal the bartender to bring more water.

I don't know Anya well but I feel responsible for her since we have so many friends in common. The fact that she has a bit of a crush on my man is a minor annoyance. Hey, it's not like I can blame her.

He is pretty dreamy.

"What do you mean?"

"You're gorgeous. You have the whole Gigi Hadid thing going on. Why are you drinking at the bar during a wedding? I mean, I know why I'm here."

"Why are you here? Aren't you the one with the hot silver fox boyfriend?"

"The man who wants to keep our relationship a secret? The man who never wants to talk about the future? Is that really a boyfriend or just a man I don't have the willpower to say no to?"

"Ahhh, I think I'm starting to understand. He won't commit. Sounds like we have opposite problems. Your guy won't stay and I can't figure out how to get rid of mine. Maybe we should switch lives."

She snorts with laughter almost falling off the barstool. Wisely, the bartender leaves her water and then quickly retreats.

Anya takes a gulp from the glass. Unfortunately most of it goes down the front of her dress. I smother a laugh.

The bartender gives me a look like *I am not taking responsibility for this one.*

"Don't say it. I know I'm a hot mess," Anya grumbles.

"No, you're just disappointed. I've been there. Men are fun to play with but you can't rely on them. You have to rely on yourself."

The words I've parroted so many times sound hollow. But this is what has gotten me through the years. Having casual, fun relationships and expecting nothing more.

It hurts because I'd really started to hope for more with Vin. I thought we could have it all. But I was just fooling myself.

"I want to rely on myself. Be all *independent woman, hear me roar!* But it never seems to work out that way. Tell me how you do it." Anya looks fascinated.

"I just do what I want. Men get away with all kinds of bad behavior but women are expected to be perfect. *So stop being perfect.* Just live your life in the moment. See that hot guy over there?"

She glances behind us. There is an extremely sexy man standing on the other side of the room.

"Wow. Yeah, he is hot."

I wink. "You should ask for his number."

"What? I can't do that. I h-have a boyfriend."

"Do you? Because I'm pretty sure you just said that dude doesn't want to be locked down."

Anya looks skeptical. "Well, what about you? You're trying to get rid of a guy, so what are you doing wrong?"

"I don't know. That's just it. None of my usual crazy is working. I've done some of the most batshit stuff to this guy and he just... rolls with it."

"You should cook for him. Ask him about his day. Kiss him like you missed him. That should send him running. It works for me."

I turn to Anya in amazement. Her drunken musings may have just solved both of our problems.

Be nice. Be clingy.

It's the ultimate power play.

"That's it. We don't switch lives. We switch methods. I'll do things the Anya way. You do things the Ariana way. We both get what we want."

She blinks. "Just start acting differently?"

"Nothing else has worked. So what have we got to lose?"

"I'm going to talk to Law. We're adults, right? We should be able to have a calm, rational discussion about what we each need from our relationship." She looks down at her phone suddenly. "Crap, I have to go."

"Good luck. And I'm not being shady when I say that. I actually hope it works out for you."

She hurries away, unaware that she's just changed my life.

I can't hurt Vin. It would kill me to do it. He's been so sweet and supportive. All I can do is the one thing guaranteed to make him leave on his own.

Act like his wife.

Til' death do us part.

It's only about ten minutes later when Vin finds me in the bar. He's unbuttoned his tuxedo jacket and looks tired. He takes a seat next to me but waves the bartender away when he approaches.

"Did Andre and Casey get off all right?"

He smiles. "They rode off into the sunset under a hail of rice and good wishes."

His description makes it easy to picture. Everything about this wedding was straight from a fairytale. The handsome prince. The small-town girl. Hell, there had even been a villain. I laugh again thinking of the girl in the rogue wedding dress I'd chased off earlier.

Vin looks at my empty glass. "Are you ready to go?"

"Yes. I am. It's been a long day." One I really don't want to finish alone. "Will you come home with me tonight?"

His eyes search mine. "Is that what you want?"

He's really asking if I've considered what staying means. Whether I'm ready for more. But we've reached a point where it's all about to fall to pieces anyway and I need the memory of our last night together to be a good one.

"I want you to stay."

"Then I'll stay." He kisses me lightly and then offers his arm. We walk together back to the grand ballroom. It looks like a tornado ran through it.

"I feel bad about missing the bouquet toss."

He inclines his head. "Do you? Really?"

I can't help smiling. He always calls me on my bullshit.

"Not really but I feel like I *should* feel bad. Does that count? Casey should have had all her girls cheering her on."

"I doubt she noticed. There was a whole herd of squawking women competing to catch that bouquet. I saw some elbows being thrown. It was a brawl."

"You're making that up."

"Someone's hair extension hit the floor. It looked like a blond rat."

"You're *definitely* making that up."

"Did it make you feel better?"

"Slightly."

When I get to my apartment, I immediately slip out of my dress and hang it in the closet. It's doubtful I'll ever wear it again (*who first came up with that lie about people being able to wear their bridesmaid dresses again?*) but it's still really expensive. The fabric alone is worth more than anything else in my closet. It seems wrong to just throw it over a chair.

After giving Oreo some obligatory belly rubs, I start cleaning up the mess I left in the kitchen this morning. Time got away from me and I had to leave without cleaning up from breakfast. It's a good distraction while I wait for Vin to show up.

We couldn't leave together since that would defeat the whole point of keeping our relationship undercover. Plus, he'd mentioned having to run up to his room at the hotel really quickly to grab a change of clothes. But that should have only taken about fifteen minutes.

As the time ticks away, I rub my chest. This is starting to feel way too similar to the times my mom would promise to come visit and never show up. It's been two hours since we left the reception and it doesn't take that long to get here from the hotel, even with Saturday night traffic.

Maybe I won't even need to implement Operation Wifey since he seems to have already forgotten about me.

Quickest plan ever.

I scoop up Oreo, cuddling my face into her soft fur. "It's okay, girl. I guess it's just us."

I know she'll be just as disappointed. She's still a little skittish when Vin pets her but she seems to really like sleeping at his feet. Or next to him on the couch.

Just when I'm about to go to bed, there's a knock at the door. I run back and fling it open.

Vin pauses when he sees the look on my face. Then he smiles in that way of his, that infuriating way, that says he knows what I'm thinking.

The fact that he's usually right makes it worse.

"You thought I forgot?"

I shrug like it doesn't matter but I step back so he can come in.

"Casey texted me and asked me to come by. They're leaving for their honeymoon tomorrow and she wanted to say goodbye."

"Casey wanted to say goodbye? Not your brother?"

He picks me up making me squeal. "My brother's got his dream girl. I don't think he even noticed I was there."

When we reach my room, he sets me down on my feet. For a long moment, he just stares at me.

"What is it?"

"Just taking you in. I've been waiting for this a long time."

Knowing how the next day is going to go, I feel guilty. "You've been waiting a long time to listen to me snore? For me to kick you all night?"

"To be able to hold you all night." He kisses my forehead.

He follows me into the bathroom and while I brush my teeth, he sets a few of his things on the bathroom counter. Watching him line up his toothbrush and toothpaste there makes me sad.

Because after a few days of what I have planned, I'll never see them again.

He brushes his teeth quickly and then follows me back into the bedroom. I jump in on my usual side on the right. He strips down to his boxers before getting in next to me.

"Tired?" he asks.

"Exhausted."

"Me too. If I ever get married, remind me to do it in front of Elvis and skip all this crap."

"I promise." I lean over and turn the light off before he can see how his words affect me. Just because he won't be around soon doesn't mean I won't miss him. And the day he marries someone else is the day my heart breaks for good.

He slides closer, wrapping his arms around me from behind. I won't be able to sleep like this for long because his body already feels like a furnace but for now, it feels good.

"Ariana?" he whisper-yells.

"Yes?" I whisper back.

"I got my dream girl, too."

18

Din

WAKING UP WITH THE ONE YOU LOVE IS AN experience everyone should be privileged to have. I've been looking forward to it. Over the years I've dated casually and even spent the night with a few of the women. But when morning came it was always an awkward dance to put my clothes back on and get the hell out of there.

With Ariana, I've fantasized about holding her close. About burying my nose in her hair, breathing her scent and listening to her heartbeat.

So imagine my surprise when I open my eyes the next morning to an empty bed.

"Ari? Where are you, woman?"

The door opens and in walks a vision with tousled hair and rosy cheeks. She's wearing nothing but my dress shirt and a smile. Is there anything sexier than a woman wearing your clothes? All my blood is busy going south so it takes me a minute to process what I'm seeing.

And what I'm smelling.

"I made you breakfast." She sets the tray she's holding carefully over my lap. Then with a snap of her wrist, unfolds a paper napkin that she rests against my stomach.

"What's all this?"

She smiles sweetly. "Just a little something I whipped up."

Whipped up? Ariana has made no secret of her disdain for household tasks. During all the time we've spent together the only cooking I've seen her do is putting a bag of popcorn in the microwave. Wary now, I peer down at the tray in concern.

"You made this? I thought you didn't cook?"

Ariana scowls for a second. Then she pastes on another bright smile. "I said I hated cooking. Not that I couldn't do it. Eat up!"

I take a tentative bite of the eggs and am surprised at the fluffy, creamy texture. The bacon is crisp and the coffee smells fantastic. The tray is beautifully arranged with a full assortment of silverware next to the plate. She's even placed a single rose to the side.

It's all so perfect that I'm instantly suspicious.

"Thank you for breakfast."

Still smiling like a loon, Ariana claps her hands together. "I'm so happy you're enjoying it. My man needs to keep his strength up!"

I take another bite of eggs while watching her bustle around the room straightening up. Ariana keeps things relatively neat but she's never cared about whether clothes are in the middle of the floor before. It's unsettling, watching her flit around like this.

Maybe she's about to tell me her test results. I didn't bring it up last night because it's her news to share. She should be able to tell me when she's ready. Making breakfast may have been her way of easing into the conversation.

I push the tray to the side and give her my full attention.

"What's going on, baby? You're full of energy this morning."

She pulls a sweatshirt out of the closet and yanks it over her head. "We have a lot to do today. Didn't I tell you? I *really* need to go shopping."

"Shopping?" This is so far from what I expected her to say that I'm experiencing mental whiplash.

"Yes. Shopping. I would love for you to come with me. I'm so lucky to have a boyfriend now. Someone to vote on my outfits and tell me if my ass looks too big in each one!"

My mind is scrambling looking for a way out. That sounds awful and it's exactly the kind of game that no man can win. If you say a woman looks good in everything they claim you aren't paying attention. If you say something looks bad, then expect sulking for the rest of the night.

"You need me to go shopping? Isn't that something you'd rather do by yourself?"

Her expression doesn't change.

"Of course not, silly! I mean, we're together now, right?" At my nod, she beams. "This is one of those things that couples do together. I'm so excited to do all the coupley-things!"

She's talking so animatedly that I can't stand the idea of interrupting her. But I'm still mentally reeling from this complete flip in her personality that seems to have happened overnight.

When we went to sleep, she seemed like her normal self.

Now she's cooking and clapping and excited to go shopping? What the hell happened while I was asleep?

"You know I would do anything for you. If you want to go shopping, I guess we'll go shopping."

Ariana squeals. "Yay! Hurry up and get ready. I can't wait to take you to all of my favorite boutiques so you can watch me try on everything."

"Maybe not everything," I mumble.

She claps her hands again and levels me with a look. The intensity in her eyes scares me a little.

"Everything."

Three hours later, I'm about ready to tap out.

When Ariana said everything, she really meant every fucking thing in every fucking boutique in DC.

But every time I'm about to tell her we should go home, she looks at me with those big, hazel eyes and I can't do it. She's so happy right now. How can I take that away?

"Here we are!" Ariana crows excitedly, dragging me by the arm toward yet another store.

"You're not tired at all, huh?" I'm hoping that at some point her feet will start to hurt or she'll get hungry.

"Oh no. I'm just getting started."

With that terrifying statement, she drags me through the door and straight toward the nearest sales associate.

The woman must be experienced because with one head-to-toe look, she's clearly seen enough to decide that we're serious shoppers. Maybe it's the material of my linen shirt or the maniacal glee in Ariana's eyes that tips her off. Then again it could be the huge shopping bags that Ariana is banging into everything that lets her know we won't be a waste of her time.

"Hello. Welcome to Rapture. My name is Meredith. Is there anything I can assist you with today?"

Ariana squeezes my arm. "Yes. My hubby here is treating me to a shopping day. Isn't that just the sweetest?"

My head whips to the side. *Hubby?* That's new. On one hand I'm thrilled that she seems on board with this new direction in our relationship. When she invited me to stay the night for the first time, I was hopeful that it meant we could move forward. But this is completely unexpected.

The saleswoman's eyes sparkle. "How generous. Are you looking for anything in particular?"

"Surprise me," Ariana purrs before dragging me toward the dressing rooms.

Before long the saleswoman reappears with an entire rack of dresses. My eyes widen at the amount of clothes. There's no way I can let Ariana try on all of that. We'll be here all day.

"These are some of our newest arrivals. There's a cashmere sweater dress that I think you will *love*." Meredith parks the rack next to the dressing room Ariana has claimed.

By the wolfish expression in her eyes, I have a feeling Meredith *loves* the prospect of a very large commission.

For the next ten minutes, Ariana tries on outfit after outfit, coming out of the dressing room to model each one. My head drops to my hands in agony as she reenters the dressing room for the fifth time.

None of this makes sense.

Underneath the door I see a dress hit the floor. Ari steps out of it and I'm hit with an image of her naked behind those doors, her beautiful body reflecting in all the mirrors.

My lips curl up into a diabolical grin.

I have no idea what kind of game my *wifey* is playing but I know something that would make it a lot more fun for me.

Meredith is at the front counter when I approach. There's only one other person in the boutique, an older woman near the front trying on a scarf.

"Would you mind being really busy with other customers for about ten minutes?" Palming my wallet, I comb through the bills before handing her a hundred dollars.

She whistles. "What do you know? I really need to rearrange that front window display. That should take ages."

Satisfied that we won't be interrupted, I go back to the dressing room area. Ariana should be out again soon with another outfit for me to vote on. All I have to do is bide my time. Sure enough, about sixty seconds later the door to her dressing room opens. Before she can step out, I slide past her.

"Vin, what are you doing?"

My arm curls around her waist and I swing her around so the door to the dressing room can close. The outfit she's wearing is a sparkly black dress with long balloon sleeves. It emphasizes her small waist and those mile long legs. She looks amazing as always.

But she'd look even better out of it.

At the first kiss on her neck, she stiffens.

"Vin! We can't. The saleslady will be back any minute."

My hands slide beneath her dress to grip her ass, squeezing the soft globes gently.

"The saleslady is really happy about the commission she's about to earn. Since your *hubby* is paying for everything."

She looks guilty for about a split second before her chin sets in the mulish expression I've come to love.

Oh yes, my girl is up to something. I may not have figured out exactly what it is yet, but I plan to have fun with it in the meantime.

"It's cute to have nicknames for each other," Ari says.

"You won't mind if I call you wifey then?"

She looks horrified. I bury my face in her neck to hide my amusement. There's definitely a reason she's acting like a brainless twit but it's going to be so much fun to get it out of her.

"You want to call me that?"

"Oh yes, it'll be like a game. I happen to love games. Especially the one where the hubby fucks his little wifey in the dressing room where anyone can hear."

She shudders in my arms. "We can't. Can we?"

It's obvious she wants to despite the fact that I'm throwing a wrench in whatever her little scheme is supposed to be.

Not even the idea of being overheard deters her. It drives me crazy how much my girl loves to be bad.

"Doesn't the little wifey want to take care of her man? She has what he needs. A sweet little spot that he loves to taste."

Her fingers clench on my arm that's wrapped around her waist. She moans and I bite her right on the throat, knowing she loves a little pain with her pleasure. Sure enough, she grinds back on me, rubbing her bottom on the hard bulge poking her in the back.

"Bend over baby. Hold on to the bench."

No longer trying to pretend like she's not into it, Ariana leans over eagerly, the move thrusting her bottom toward me. I flip up the fabric of the dress and then hook a finger in the material covering her pussy. It's a thong so it doesn't take much to move it out of my way. Then I replace it with my tongue.

Ari squirms as I lick her gently before giving her pussy a hard, suctioning kiss. Before long she's moving with me, shamelessly riding my tongue. She whines when I stop circling her sweet little hole and turn her around. Her cheeks are red and her blond hair is all over her face.

"Take them off," I growl, too far gone to wait any longer. Whatever game we were playing just got real.

She holds my gaze as she peels the panties down her legs. I unbutton my pants and shove everything down to the floor. I get a condom on faster than I ever have, too turned on to waste a second.

"Come here, baby. You started this. Now it's time to finish it." I pick her up and brace her against the wall.

Her eyes flash, defiant to the last. "I started it? You came in here."

"I'm pretty sure you knew that would happen after you've made me look at that delectable body for the past few hours."

She moans as I rock against her. I don't even need to guide my cock in, she's so wet it finds home with no trouble. I grit my teeth at the pleasure. Every time it's like my dick is being squeezed and massaged in a rapid rhythm.

"My wifey knows what I need," I taunt and am rewarded when she tightens her internal muscles even more, making my breath stutter in my chest.

"Does she?"

"Yes. She knows I just need her. That's all I need, baby."

Her eyes close and I speed up, unable to hold back any longer. I'm sure everyone outside this room knows what we're doing because with each thrust, we slam against the wall and Ariana lets out a hoarse little cry. Then her hands tighten in my hair and I know she's about to come.

I cover her mouth with mine as I finally let go and let my own orgasm overtake me. We shudder together for what seems like an eternity before I finally allow her feet to touch the ground.

"There's no way she didn't hear that," Ariana whispers.

"Are you kidding? She probably has her ear to the door right now."

Ariana glances at the door to the dressing room and then gives me a dirty look. "Don't even joke about that. That's so weird."

I don't have a tissue so I just knot the condom and wrap it in one of the flyers the boutique has put in each dressing room.

Ariana sighs. "Give it to me. I'll put it in my purse. It's bad enough that everyone heard us but you can't walk out there with a huge ball of crinkled up paper in your pocket."

We laugh together at the absurdity of that mental image.

When we come out a few minutes later, Meredith averts her eyes politely. Ariana runs a hand self-consciously over her wild hair, trying to smooth it down. I'm sure mine is standing on end as well but I don't even bother to fix it.

Completely unashamed, I drag Ariana up to the counter.

"My wife loved it. We'll take it all."

19

Ariana

WHEN WE GET HOME, VIN DEPOSITS ALL THE BAGS IN my room and comes back out. He was extremely cheerful all the way home meanwhile I'm still walking bowlegged after being pounded against the wall.

I'm not sure how I lost control of that situation but I have to own it. That was a complete disaster. It was hot as hell, obviously, but it's not what I expected to happen. The point of that little shopping excursion was to torment him. I'd figured he'd make up an excuse to leave after the first hour, claiming a work emergency or a water main break at his brother's penthouse or a sudden urge to get a dental cleaning.

Instead he'd turned the entire situation on its head. I'll never think of shopping the same way again.

Damn it.

Maybe I should have put more thought into this plan. I didn't consider last night that Vin is as unpredictable as I am. There's no way I could have guessed he'd be so into the whole hubby and wifey thing. *Really* into it. I shift in my seat. My pussy is still tingling.

Maybe I'm going about this all wrong. In retrospect I can see how that shopping scenario might be a tad too close to a porno scene. Of course he'd taken it there. He's a guy. I'd given him the perfect opening by undressing in a room a few feet away from him.

I won't make that mistake again.

No, I need to remind him of the annoying, everyday stuff that comes with living with someone. The stuff that's impossible to romanticize.

I glance over at Vin. He's just gotten comfortable on the other end of the couch. He leans back and stretches his legs out. His head falls back on the cushion with a huge sigh. He's probably tired from all that walking. I can relate because my feet are killing me.

I bet the last thing he wants to do right now is get up.

"Vin? Sweetums?"

He grunts.

"Can you get me a glass of water?"

The *are you kidding me* look he sends my way makes my chest hurt from suppressed laughter. But the whole point is to be annoying so I make a puppy dog face.

"*Please?* I'm so thirsty. It was a lot of work trying on all those clothes."

He heaves out a sigh and then gets to his feet. He trudges into the kitchen and bends down to look in the refrigerator. He comes back with a water bottle. I wait until he's almost back to the couch before I make an exaggerated disgusted face.

"Oh no. I can't drink *those* water bottles."

He looks at it in confusion. "But they're in your fridge."

"They're not for me. Those are for guests. I only drink the... organic, vitamin water infused with ginseng." It's a struggle to keep a straight face.

"Organic water?" The look he sends me this time is murderous.

"Only the best for your wifey!"

When he turns to go back to the kitchen, I call out "Thank you, honey!"

He brings back the can of organic gross water that Mya brought by a few weeks ago and forgot to take with her. I take the can and open it, making a huge production out of taking a sip. It's so disgusting that it's a struggle not to make a face.

I give him a thumbs-up.

"That is perfect. Thank you baby. It's so nice to have a man around the house."

"I'll bet," he responds drily.

After he gets settled on the couch, I decide not to ask him to get up again. Even I'm not that evil. He should at least be comfortable while I'm torturing him.

Being annoying is harder than I thought it would be. I'm running out of things to do. What do women normally do that men hate? Discreetly, I do a web search on my phone. The first hit is an article from a major women's magazine. I click through and start reading the entries.

People actually do this stuff?

I close the article. I'm not going to the bathroom in front of him. Even I have to draw the line somewhere.

I pick up the remote. Maybe I can find one of those Housewives marathons. If that doesn't push him over the edge, I don't know what will. But when I turn on the TV, Netflix pops up.

One of the categories catches my eye.

"Let's watch a movie! That always puts me in a good mood."

"Excellent. Yes, let's do that."

He sounds so relieved that I have to smother my laugh with another sip of water. Except I forgot it was Mya's gross water and the taste takes me off guard. I choke and droplets spill over my lips landing on the front of my shirt.

Vin watches me knowingly. "It must be good, huh? The organic water that you only had one can of."

"Mmm hmm. It's so good."

I turn my head to cover my gagging and use the remote to hit the movie I want.

"The Baker's Christmas Cupcake?" Vin reads one of the titles before turning horrified eyes in my direction.

"Maybe we should watch that one. That looks so sweet!"

"You want to watch a Christmas movie?" He swallows audibly. "It's September."

Jackpot.

I give myself a mental pat on the back. Sappy, romantic comedies that look like Santa threw up all over them are guaranteed to make him run for the hills.

"It's never too early for a heartwarming tale about a small-town baker!"

He doesn't respond as I eagerly click the movie and snuggle up next to him. As the opening music plays over a montage of a woman walking through the snow and smiling up at a bakery sign, I grab a throw blanket and get comfortable.

An hour later, I nod off for the third time. When my chin hits my chest again, I jerk up.

Vin is still wide awake. He watches me wipe the drool off my chin with a smirk.

"I was going to let you tell me on your own but I can't take this any longer."

"What?"

"Your test results. They must have been bad or you would have told me. Is that why you've been acting so strangely all day?"

Stunned, I can only nod.

"And I can only guess that you figured being extremely weird would make me get annoyed and leave you so you wouldn't have to tell me."

Tears gather at the edge of my lids. "Operation Wifey was clearly a failure."

Vin immediately pulls me into his embrace, burying his face in my hair. "You crazy woman. Haven't you figured it out by now? I'm in love with you. Being weird isn't going to get rid of me."

As usual, his understanding fills me with gratitude and wonder. He holds me for a little longer, giving me time to wipe away my tears with the edge of the blanket.

Since I'm in no shape to explain anything, I pull up the voicemail from Dr. Rose and let him listen to it.

"Your test is tomorrow?"

I nod. "Yeah. She scheduled a bunch of tests for Monday afternoon. That was as soon as she could get me in."

"Okay. So we're going for testing tomorrow."

When he sees the look on my face, his eyes narrow and he gets that dark, intense look I love.

"We are going for testing tomorrow."

"I feel so bad about taking you away from work. It's right in the middle of the day."

He shakes his head. "Ariana, I can take off from work. Especially for something important. *You* are important."

Suddenly he tilts his head. "Is this why you work part-time through an agency? So you don't have to worry about needing time off for tests and appointments?"

I nod. "I was in college when I first got diagnosed. I had to finish my degree part-time. I like the agency. They've been really great and I have the flexibility to study for the RN exam. It's hard to make plans when you aren't sure what's going to happen. Every scan, I worried the cancer would be back. Why?"

"Nothing. A lot of things are starting to make sense now, that's all."

I rest my head against his chest feeling relieved and also a little shy. But I can't deny that I'm so glad he knows now.

No matter what happens next, I'm not alone.

"You really think you have me all figured out now."

Vin smiles and picks up the remote. "Not quite. But I'm definitely going to get you back by making you watch the rest of this boring movie."

I try to grab the remote and shriek with laughter when he tickles my ribs.

"Take your punishment, Ari. You are going to watch this woman make her magical Christmas cupcakes!"

In the end, we did finish watching the Christmas movie only because Vin enjoyed making fun of almost every single scene.

"This is going to be our first Christmas tradition of the year. We'll watch one of these horrible movies together while I try to convince you to make out with me on the couch."

"Not that you'll have to try that hard," I reply, touched at the idea of us having our own Christmas traditions.

Having someone who wants to be around that long is still new for me. I suspect being loved so sweetly is going to take some getting used to.

There's a loud series of knocks at the door. We both look at each other.

"Are you expecting anyone?" Vin asks, before walking over to look through the peephole.

"No. Is it Mya?"

He shakes his head. Then whisper-yells, "It's an older lady. A blonde. And a whole lot of suitcases."

"Older! Young man did you just say *older*? The nerve!"

I drop the remote and rush to the door. Vin has to step back so I can open it.

"Mom?"

"Darling! There you are! Oh, you look so beautiful, even in these awful cotton pajamas." My mother rushes into the room and drags me into a heavily-fragranced hug.

Vin looks on with amusement until one of the suitcases she's dragging rolls over his bare foot.

"Ow! *Madre di—*"

She looks over at him sharply as if offended that his foot got in the way of her bag. "And who is this?"

I heave a sigh. "Mom, this is Philippe Lavin. Vin, this is my mother Ingrid Larsson."

"It's a pleasure," he pants, still holding his toe.

"Charmed." Ingrid thrusts her carryon bag in my direction. Then she pauses to look at Vin. "Lavin? Darling, didn't your roommate marry a Lavin?"

I put an arm around my mom's shoulders and steer her toward the living room.

"Mom, you really should sit down and drink something. Those airplanes are so dry. And all that recirculated air is so bad for the complexion."

As expected my comment redirects her attention. She immediately sits on the couch and pulls her water bottle from her bag.

I whip around and face Vin. "I am so sorry."

"Don't be. I'm starting to see why you're such a force of nature."

"Force of nature is a very kind way to put it. I had no idea she planned to show up tonight."

"I can tell."

"Please don't be offended but could you come back tomorrow? I can't sleep with you knowing my mother is on the other side of the wall. And yes, I know it's ridiculous because I'm a grown woman but still."

"Ari, no explanation is needed. Spend some time with your mother. I'll go catch up on some work. It's no problem."

After a quick kiss and a detour to the bedroom, Vin comes out carrying his overnight bag. He waves to my mother who pretends she doesn't see him. He chuckles.

"The test tomorrow, are you sure you still want to come? That was before I knew my mom would be here."

He gathers me closer. "I won't come if it makes you uncomfortable but I'd rather be there than at work wondering what's going on. Do *you* want me there?"

"I do. It's kind of selfish I guess. It's not like I'll be alone this time. And it means you'll be in the waiting room with my mother for *hours*."

"It's not selfish. I'll come back in the morning and bring your mom breakfast. I know you can't eat beforehand but it'll give me a chance to get to know my future mother-in-law." He smirks.

I roll my eyes at that. He's never going to let me live that *hubby* comment down.

"Okay. Bye." I kiss him quickly but I should have expected more. This is my man we're talking about after all. He bends me over his arm and gives me the kind of kiss that would make a nun want to sin.

"See you tomorrow, wifey."

20

Din

SLEEPING WITH ARI HAS RUINED SLEEPING ALONE FOR
me. Since I'm awake early, I decide to tackle some work.
Working around Ariana's tests and appointments will have
to become my new norm.

That's something I can't contemplate just yet so instead I
answer emails.

Once it hits eight o'clock, I figure it's late enough. I didn't
want to show up at Ariana's place too early and wake them

M. MALONE

up. That definitely wouldn't help me make a better impression on her mother.

Although I have a feeling nothing will help in that department. Ingrid appears to be one of those people that can find fault with anything.

After a quick pit stop to buy an assortment of pastries and several types of coffee, I drive to Ariana's apartment. At this time of morning on a weekday parking spaces are actually available near her building. I'm grateful since I'm sure her mom will be annoyed if the coffee is cold.

I knock three times. After a few minutes I knock again. A door down the hall swings open and an old lady with curlers in her hair looks out.

"Could you be any louder?" she yells in a thin, reedy voice. "Asshole." The last part is muttered as she slams her door.

The door in front of me opens finally and Ingrid regards me with interest. "Oh, hello. I wondered when you'd be back. Come in. Come in."

She turns and walks away, leaving the door open so I can follow. Perplexed by her much friendlier demeanor, I follow her inside. Her long, silky robe swirls around her legs as she takes a seat at the kitchen counter. With her blond hair and blue eyes, it's like looking at a paler version of her daughter. She really is a beautiful woman.

"I brought some food and coffee, ma'am."

"Thank you. So mannerly. My daughter has been keeping you a secret."

I'm not sure how to respond to that. But Ingrid doesn't appear to need my input to the conversation.

"Ariana wouldn't give me any of the juicy details but I already read all about the wedding online. The pictures look like heaven." She takes a tentative sip of one of the coffees before putting it down and taking another. After another sip, she apparently deems this one acceptable before she opens the box of pastries.

I have to hold back a smile as she makes faces at each one before finally making a selection.

"It was a beautiful wedding. My brother and Casey are very happy. They're on their honeymoon."

"I bet it's somewhere tropical. That's the life. I told Ariana she missed her chance. That roommate of hers got to the prize first." She taps my arm playfully. "But it looks like my daughter bounced back. The second brother isn't so bad."

The piece of croissant I've been absently chewing gets stuck in my throat. I cough to clear it. Ingrid jumps at the loud sound.

"Sorry. You said... Ariana used to talk about Andre?"

Ingrid laughs. "Oh yes. She told me when her roommate bagged him. The way she talked about it, I think she was quite jealous."

Unsure where to look, I take a sip of coffee so I don't have to respond. Ingrid keeps talking but nothing she's saying registers. Instead my mind is going over all the early conversations I had with Ariana. She admits to yelling at Andre and slamming the door on him. But was that their only interaction?

I was under the impression she barely knew him. Now that I think about it, there's no way that can be true. How much time did Andre spend here before he convinced Casey to move in with him? Suddenly I'm envisioning Andre hanging out in this very kitchen while Ariana secretly lusted after him.

Then I remember how she acted back when we first met. She was pushing me away but didn't actually ghost me until she found out my last name. Was it really out of concern for her friend's career or was it because I wasn't the Lavin she wanted to target? Maybe she thought it was better to avoid me so she'd have time to try to get to Andre.

Was I just the consolation prize she settled for after Andre got engaged?

I wrap the croissant I've been tearing to shreds in a napkin and throw it away.

"Can you tell Ari that I had to go? I just...have to go."

Ingrid pauses mid-sentence and frowns. "Well, I–"

Without waiting to hear whatever else she's about to say, I take my coffee and leave. It's better if I go now before I say anything I can't take back.

I sit in the back of the cab, ignoring the driver's attempts at polite conversation. Going to work is the only thing I can focus on right now.

At least I know what I'm doing there.

When I enter the office, Cheryl looks up and smiles. "Morning! I wasn't expecting to see you today."

"Change of plans. I need everything on the NBA deal. And the latest updates on the ready-to-wear line."

She nods, obviously sensing my mood. I go into my office and shut the door. As I sit behind the desk, my hands shake slightly. Being here isn't as neutral as I thought. Even this office carries so many memories that are all entwined with Ariana.

All the times I pulled that napkin out of my desk to look at it after she ghosted. The exploding dick bomb and all the meetings I daydreamed my way through while thinking about her. There's no part of my life she hasn't touched at some point.

A new email pops up. Cheryl has already forwarded the files I need. Introducing a more affordable line of menswear has been my pet project and lately I've been neglecting it. At least now I'll have a chance to catch up. I'm sure Ari won't miss me being there this morning. She has her mother with her. They're probably laughing about my quick departure. I groan and resolve to focus. But after reading the newest report from my manager of domestic sales, all I can do is bang my head on the desk.

Cheryl knocks and then opens the door. "Everything okay?"

"Perfect. Except sales teams are having trouble getting placement for the ready-to-wear line because the price is still too high."

"Do you want to talk about it?"

"I am talking about it," I grumble.

She harrumphs. "I have three sons. I know brooding when I see it."

"Everything is falling apart. I feel like I can't get it right. The new line can't get traction. My girl...that's not going to work. Andre will come back from vacation and find his company in the trash."

Cheryl closes the door behind her.

"Everything isn't falling apart. This company is thriving. You are the driving force behind so many changes. Who first came up with the idea for Andre to design for Hollywood? You. Who is the one who pushed him to consider a ready-to-wear line? You."

Her words soothe a sore spot I hadn't realized was still there. Years ago, I recognized my brother's skyrocketing fame had stirred up some old feelings of insecurity from my childhood. I'd dealt with it, or so I thought.

But hearing Cheryl point out all the contributions I thought no one had noticed, means I'm not as evolved as I'd hoped. I shouldn't need outside validation for the things I know I bring to the table.

"I guess that's true."

She smiles kindly. "You have such high standards that you perceive success as business as usual and only notice the things that *don't* work. I'm willing to bet you do the same thing in your personal life. You need to give yourself a break."

"Thank you, Cheryl." Emotion makes my voice gruff.

"Your brother trusts you because you have good sense and his best interest at heart. One of the few people who sees him as a person and not an entity. Maybe you should examine why you don't trust yourself."

With that one final gem of wisdom, she opens the door.

"Cheryl?"

She turns back.

"Run away with me. Let's leave it all behind."

Her laughter fills the room.

"The only place I'm running is home at exactly five o'clock. My family is visiting with the grandkids and I have a houseful of boys to cook for. My Charlie is a sweetheart but he can't boil water."

After the door closes, I ponder her words. She's right, as usual. Solving problems is one of my specialties.

Leaning forward, I start a new email. If we can find alternate fabric suppliers and get a lower cost, we'll have a better chance to hit the numbers the fashion buyers want to see in our new line. Maybe Andre can even alter his designs slightly to make use of the less expensive fabric in places where it's not visible.

Satisfied with the potential compromise, I sit back wishing I could talk to Andre again. But there's no way I'm interrupting his honeymoon for my problems.

Plus, I already know what he'd say.

If she's the one, teach her to love.

Be the man she needs.

As Cheryl pointed out earlier, I have a tendency to only notice the negative. Ariana is honest almost to a fault. I laugh. She's so quick to tell someone to fuck off that there's no way she could spend all that time with me if she didn't really want to be there.

With her, I never felt second best. She defends me even to myself. Not to mention that she's told me before about her mother's selfishness and her tendency to twist things around to her benefit. Anything that woman says is likely to be her own interpretation of events and not based on anything Ariana ever said.

I believe in Ari. And she believes in me.

A quick glance at the clock shows I have just enough time. I race out of my office and hit the button for the elevator several times. It seems to take an eternity before the doors open. My heart is in my throat all the way down to the parking garage. I don't drive in the city often because it's just easier to grab a cab but this is one time I'm glad I did.

The ride out to Virginia is spent with one eye on the clock. What the hell is wrong with me? I imagine Ari sitting in that dismal office with only her mother to keep her calm. Who is going to tell her something funny to take her mind off the tests? Who is going to hold her hand so she doesn't feel alone?

I should have been there.

When I park in front of the building, her appointment time has already passed. I push through the doors into the waiting room and groan when I spot Ingrid sitting alone. I'm too late. They've already taken Ariana for her tests.

"What are you doing here?" Ingrid regards me icily. "You have some nerve upsetting my daughter before her tests!"

The other people in the waiting room look between us, some of them looking eager to witness a verbal showdown. I don't begrudge them their nosiness. If I had to sit in here on a regular basis, I would welcome a distraction, too.

"I love Ariana. And I'm not going anywhere. You might as well get used to it."

"Vin?"

At the sound of Ari's voice I turn around, my eyes scanning the section of the room behind the door. She's standing in the far corner holding a paper cup of water. I see relief in her eyes before they well with tears.

"I didn't think you were coming," she admits softly.

"That's because I'm an idiot. But that's a story for another time.

My thumbs brush away the tears on her cheeks. My beautiful little troublemaker should never have a reason to cry.

"I'll always show up. Even when I mess up. Even when it hurts. I'll always be here when you need me."

At the sound of her name being called, we both turn. I kiss her gently. "Go. I'll be right out here."

She squeezes my hand. "Can you come with me this time?"

"I can do that."

My words may not be able to make this process any less invasive but hopefully I can make her laugh. That's what she needs right now.

"We'll get through it together. Do you need a breast exam? If so, I can help with that part."

Her laughter tells me I got it right.

21

Ariana

THE TESTS TAKE LONGER THIS TIME. I'M SO GRATEFUL when we're done and I can leave. My mom is quiet on the way home as if she senses my need to think. Vin is following in his car and I drive fast, more than ready to be home curled up with him on the couch.

He was a real trooper holding my hands in between tests and keeping me calm by telling funny stories about his brother and his assistant at work.

I can't wait to know all the people in his life.

I can't wait to be in his life everyday.

When we reach the apartment, it doesn't take long for us to both find parking spaces and we meet at the front of the building. We climb the stairs to the third floor in silence, our shoes clattering on the stairs. By the time we get to the top, my mom is already there since she took the elevator.

I open the door so my mom can go in and sit down. Before Vin follows, I tug on his arm.

"Can you wait for me in the bedroom? I want to talk to my mom for a minute?"

Understanding shines in his eyes. "Just come get me when you're done."

Going through all the testing today gave me a lot of time to think about what I wanted to say. My mom has disappointed me a lot over the years but I can't ignore the times she's helped me either.

When I was first diagnosed, she insisted I have my surgery in Beverly Hills. I thought it was so she could make sure I used her plastic surgeon. However, thinking back, I remember how she took care of me. It couldn't have been easy to watch her only child go through that.

She's not nurturing and that's something I've come to accept. It's actually less hurtful to realize this is just the way she is.

My mom looks up when I sit next to her on the couch. "I'm sorry if I ran your young man off."

"It's okay, Mom. I just wanted to thank you for coming. It really does help having family there."

She grabs my hand and holds it on the couch cushion in between us. We sit in silence for a moment, both of us seeming unsure how to start.

"I had a lot of time to think in that waiting room today," she finally says. "And I didn't like what I realized."

My first instinct is to deny that anything is wrong, to smooth things over since that's what I always do. Then I stop and focus on just listening. It's time we actually talked to each other instead of at each other. It's the only way we'll have a relationship that goes deeper than voicemails.

"I'm sorry, Ariana. I haven't been there for you. All I could see were my own fears. I guess I thought if I pretended nothing was happening, I wouldn't have to deal with it."

Although her distance has hurt, I can see it from her perspective, too. My mom knows she's not perfect and she can admit her faults. I need to do the same.

"I'm sorry, too. When this all happened, I really didn't spend a lot of time thinking about how it would feel on your end. I was just focused on how scary it was for me."

"That's what you should have been focused on. And I should have been there more. I'm the mother. Even if I've never been very good at it. My own mother wasn't all that warm either."

She smiles. "Your young man really came through for you today though."

Just the thought of Vin makes my cheeks flush.

"Yes, he did."

"I've never had anyone I could trust like that. I got used to doing things on my own and taught you to do the same. Men weren't to be trusted. That's the only life lesson I felt I could pass on to you."

"I'm sorry if you don't get it, Mom. But I like having someone in my life that I can lean on."

She squeezes my hand to stop my rant. "I do get it. I'm lonely, Ariana. I was never good with people, not the way you are. Now I've gotten so used to being on my own that I don't think I can change. The only person I have to talk to is your father. And we drive each other crazy."

"I didn't realize you were lonely, Mom. I thought you loved your life in Beverly Hills."

She shrugs delicately. "It's what I know. People who only care what you look like and how much money you have. But I'm going to try to do better. Maybe it's not too late for me."

She pats my hand. "Now I'm going to grab my bags and go check into the Fitz. I know when I'm a third wheel."

"You don't have to leave, Mom."

"There was a time when I was young, too. And I think you need time alone with that handsome man more than anything else. Maybe we can have breakfast tomorrow. I'll try not to say anything offensive and we can all get to know each other better."

After a quick hug, she goes to the guest room to gather her things. A half hour later she's gone with a promise to call in the morning.

We spend the rest of the day watching Netflix and being lazy on the couch, Oreo happily curled at our feet. Neither of us wants to talk about the potential outcome of the tests so instead we pretend it's any other day.

Maybe that's not the healthiest approach but it makes me feel better. For just a little while, I can forget about my troubles and just be a girl spending time with her guy.

"You know, you totally ruined my plans," I tell him later that night.

He left briefly to get more clothes and now he's rocking nothing but a pair of pajama pants. His chest is bare and I'm enjoying the view. I'm wearing my favorite nightshirt as usual and my feet are in his lap. I squirm away when he pinches my toes playfully.

"Your plan? You mean Operation Wifey." His eyes twinkle. "Please, don't ever try to be wifely again."

I hit him with one of the pillows on the back of the couch. He catches it and then silences my next attack by leaning over for a kiss. My heart still skips a beat every time he kisses me.

I hope that never changes.

"Operation Wifey is dead, never to be revived."

"Thank God for that!" Vin eyes me before trailing one hand up my leg and under my shirt. "Although I do have a particular fondness for shopping now. Maybe we should do that again."

I put the pillow over my face. "I can't ever show my face in that store again."

"I'm sure our friend Meredith wouldn't mind if we came back," he jokes.

"Anyway, I was talking about my plan in general. For years, I figured I'd be a free spirit like my mom, living alone and traveling the world. I had this theory that as long as I never let anyone too close, I couldn't get hurt. It was a point of pride for me that I was strong enough to make it on my own. I never needed anyone."

"How's that working out for you?" He looks at me and I wonder if he knows his heart is in his eyes.

"You blew my theory out of the water. It turns out that loving someone and needing them to be happy isn't so bad."

He just watches me in that quiet, intense way of his, giving me time to get the words out. Vin tells me he loves me often. He's never pressured me to say it back but I'm sure he's wondering if I truly feel the same.

Each time I try to say the words, I just can't. It's like they get stuck in my throat. That probably sounds like an excuse but give me a break.

I've never done this before.

For years I've seen permanence as scary. Hoping for more felt like tempting fate. But for once, I feel like fate might actually be on my side. Everything I've been through has led me here, after all.

"I love you, Vin. I don't know what I would do without you in my life."

The smile that spreads across his face is so radiant it takes my breath away. You'd think he's been waiting his whole life to hear those words.

"I love you, too." He leans down to kiss me, lingering like he can't get enough of the feeling.

"That shouldn't have taken so long for me to say. I'm not very good at this, I'm afraid."

When he kisses me again, I can feel his lips curl up. "I can teach you."

He stands then with me in his arms, making me shriek at the sudden movement. "Right after I rock your world again."

"Rock *my* world? Mister, I will rock *your* world!"

Din

THE ELEVATOR TAKES US UP RAPIDLY, CLIMBING closer to my brother's penthouse every second.

"This may not have been the best idea." Ariana tugs at the hem of her dress.

When I asked Andre to host a dinner so I could introduce my secret girlfriend, he'd found the whole situation amusing. Especially when I'd told him who needed to be on the guest list.

It was a big deal getting Ari to go public now. She hasn't gotten the results of her second scans back yet and I know it's constantly on her mind. It's on mine, too.

But no matter what the results say, we're a couple and that's not changing. So it's time to finally let our loved ones know we're together. We're too old for this sneaking around shit. I want everyone to know she's mine.

"It's too late to cancel now. I already told Andre we were on the way."

"You said you were bringing a guest?"

"I said I was bringing the love of my life."

"Oh. Well, that's okay then." She leans over and kisses my cheek just as the elevator doors open.

Andre is waiting in the hallway. He's wearing brushed wool trousers and a plain white dress shirt. This is his version of casual.

Ariana tugs at her dress again. She confided in me last week that she finds it intimidating to dress up in front of my brother. It's one thing to wear jeans, everyone looks pretty much the same in casual clothes, but dressing up is different.

I get it. Fashion can be intimidating. That was my experience when I first started working with Andre years ago.

I grab her hand and she gives me a grateful smile.

Andre looks at me. Then he looks at Ariana.

"I thought you said you were bring–" He pauses. It's like watching a light bulb go off. He starts laughing, his hand going to his stomach like it hurts. "This is going to be fun."

Ariana fidgets, hopping from foot to foot. We follow Andre inside. The white sectional has been moved back to make room for a large dining table. It must be new. Soft music plays overhead and I can hear the sound of voices coming from the next room. Everyone must be here. Good.

"Are they here?" Casey comes trotting out of the kitchen.

A few seconds later, Mya Taylor-Hamilton follows. "Is who here?"

"Philippe is bringing his girlfriend," Casey replies.

She stops when she notices me standing in the entryway. Then her eyes swing to Ariana.

"Oh, Ari! You're here, too? I didn't know you'd be coming. I don't think I put out enough place settings."

Andre is in the corner cracking up.

Casey looks at him, appalled. "Babe, what are you doing? You're supposed to be greeting the guests. What is Philippe's girlfriend going to think when she gets here?"

That only makes him laugh harder.

Ariana scowls.

I sigh.

Mya looks confused.

"*I'm the girlfriend!*" Ariana finally blurts out. "Geez Louise."

Casey looks between us. "Wait, all this time it was you? Andre said Philippe has been seeing someone for a long time."

"Still me," Ari deadpans.

Mya bursts into laughter. "Well, I don't think anyone saw that coming. But now I understand why we got an invitation." She looks up at her husband Milo affectionately.

Casey puts her arm around Ariana's shoulders. "Well, I think this is great. You deserve the best and Philippe is the best."

She pulls Ari into a hug. But she's standing so close that I can overhear. "You have a lot of explaining to do. At least now I understand why you didn't want me to introduce him to Anya. You were jealous."

Ari looks over at me. "I was not jealous."

I just grin at this new knowledge.

"*I wasn't.*"

"Whatever you say, baby. You know I rock your world."

She rolls her eyes. "Keep messing with me and the next dicks I send you will be attached to bodies."

The entire room explodes with laughter.

"Wait, what?" Andre's going to have a heart attack with how hard he's laughing at me.

"That sounds familiar," Milo comments.

"He's lucky she didn't deliver them in person." That comment comes from Mya. "Has she shown you her scuba diving gear yet?"

Now it's my turn to look at Ariana with new eyes. "Scuba gear?"

The blush I love to tease her about starts to climb her neck. "That's nothing."

I pull her to my side and nuzzle her hair. "That's okay, baby. You can show me when we get home. I bet you look hot in a wetsuit."

Mya gapes at us. "He's as crazy as she is."

Andre watches us with a knowing smile. I'm sure he's thinking about the advice he gave me a couple of weeks ago. Back then he didn't know who it was for but I know he remembers what he said.

Love isn't just words.

It's action.

"I would like to welcome Ariana to the family," Andre says. "My brother has always had exceptional taste."

Next to me I can feel Ariana relax. In that moment I'm so grateful to my brother for always knowing exactly what to say. I think my father would really have been proud of us in this moment. This was all he wanted, to see us happy and in love, supporting each other the way brothers should. Putting family first.

I guess we're all grown up now.

"Would anyone like a glass of wine? Or a snack?" Andre gestures for us all to move toward the couch.

Then he picks up a tray from one of the side tables and holds it right in front of my face.

"Mini-wieners perhaps?" His laughter cuts off when I punch him playfully in the stomach.

We aren't that grown up yet.

A few hours later, all the other guests have left. Ariana is with Casey looking at some new romance novels she wants to borrow. Andre and I wander over to the long sectional in the living room to watch TV while we wait for the girls to come back.

"There's never anything on," Andre comments as he scrolls through the channels.

"You should try Netflix. It's never too early for a heart-warming tale about a small-town baker."

He looks at me like I'm insane. "What?"

"Never mind. It's an inside joke."

After finding a basketball game, he leans back with a sigh. Since we just signed a provisional deal to provide suits for NBA coaches once the new line debuts, Andre has been taking a bit more interest in the game. He's always been an active guy, he just prefers outdoor pursuits like hiking and running.

He lowers the volume on the television and clears his throat.

"A little birdie whispered in my ear recently. Apparently I've neglected to tell you how much I appreciate you."

"I'm going to kill Ariana."

Andre gives me a look. "You think she'd whisper in my ear? That woman would have dragged me by the balls to apologize."

"I don't need any thanks. It's my job."

"But you do. So much of what Lavin has become is directly due to your influence. When I first got the idea to use production scrap to create clothing for the homeless, it was because of you."

Uncomfortable with his effusiveness, I smirk. "I remind you of the homeless?"

"No." He laughs and punches my shoulder. "You were talking about the new line. But your points about making clothing accessible made me think."

He sighs.

"I was so pigheaded. I didn't want to even think about simplifying designs to make ready-to-wear possible and you made me see the possibilities. All I saw was lowering the price. You saw a way to get us into new closets."

"I'm sure Casey had something to do with that, too. Or did I hallucinate you working like a madman on one of your homeless designs after you lost her?"

He nods. "She definitely changed my thinking. She wore clothes that were too small to her job interview because she couldn't afford anything else then."

I hadn't realized Casey had ever struggled financially so this is news to me. "I didn't know that."

"I knew they were too small but not that it was all she had." He waggles his eyebrows. "The man in me didn't mind them being too small."

We both laugh at that.

"But seriously, that one change in thinking has turned the direction of the company. Maybe a groom who can't afford a Lavin bridal suit will choose one from VIN."

"Vin?"

"Yes. I'm naming the new line after you."

My mouth falls open. "Andre ... I don't know what to say."

He sobers, his eyes intense.

"When we started, you didn't hesitate to sink all your money into this venture with me. When *Mamma* and *Papa* were still unsure, you were the one that said to trust me. That I would change the way the world sees design. Fashion wasn't even something you cared about but you learned to care. For me."

"You would have done the same for me."

"Of course I would have. But that doesn't make it any less extraordinary."

He claps me on the back.

"Brother, it may be my face in the ads but the name on the door belongs to both of us."

"*Papa* would be proud of us."

"Yes, he would. I'm proud of us, too. Especially you." Andre shakes his head. "When you asked me for advice, I had no idea it was for Ariana."

"Would that have changed the advice?"

"I probably would have told you to be careful. And to wear one of those protective cups over your balls."

I crack up.

"But seriously, you obviously got it right. I've never seen Ariana look so happy. She seems almost ... normal now."

The girls come back into the room then. Ariana is holding a stack of books but still manages to gesture wildly with one hand. Then she makes a movement that is clearly pantomiming giving a blow job.

Andre looks over at me. "I spoke too soon."

"Normal is boring. Besides, I wanted her to be comfortable being herself in front of all of our family and friends. That's what this dinner was about."

Andre grins. "This wasn't the family dinner you need to worry about. Wait until she meets *Mamma*."

EPILOGUE

Ariana

VIN SLIDES INTO THE KITCHEN, DANCING IN HIS SOCKS before he grabs me around the waist.

"Is it almost time?"

I look at the clock on the microwave. We invited everyone over for two o'clock so they should be here in about ten minutes.

"Not quite. I'm just making some punch. Can't have cake without punch."

He grins as I do a little wiggle.

"I love seeing you like this. So happy."

Things were tense while we waited to find out my results. Once Dr. Rose called to tell me the new tests were clear, I was so excited I dropped the phone before she finished talking. We've both been in a great mood ever since. Vin even took me to meet his mom yesterday. It wasn't exactly a lovefest but I think we'll eventually grow to be friends. Sofia Lavin may be difficult but after dealing with my parents, I can handle anything.

"Tell me again," he whisper-yells against my neck.

"I'm just fine," I whisper back.

I think he needs reassurance also. False positives happen but I never thought it would happen to me.

Once I knew the new test results were okay, Vin and I talked about my tendency to hide things from my friends. Over the years, I've thought about telling them what I was going through but it just seemed easier to deal with it alone. I didn't want anyone's pity.

I definitely didn't want cancer to be the only thing they see when they look at me. Once people know you've been sick, it's hard to get them to see anything else.

But as Vin pointed out, these aren't *people* these are my *friends*. They've known me for years and they aren't going to suddenly start treating me differently because of this.

He also asked how I would feel if I found out one of them had been sick and I never knew about it. I had to admit it wouldn't feel great to be left out.

Being with Vin has shown me how amazing it can be to open up to the people who love you. It makes every burden easier to bear and every joy is magnified.

As if he can hear my thoughts, Vin squeezes my waist. "Do you know what you're going to tell your friends?"

"I decided to be direct. Honest. Facts only."

He nods. "Good. This situation requires some emotional sensitivity though. Expect them to be shocked. Maybe even hurt."

I've prepared myself for that reaction. I expect Mya to take it the hardest. We've known each other the longest and she was living here while a lot of this was going on.

Vin squeezes my waist. "I know how it feels to find out someone you love is in danger."

"Was in danger," I correct.

"Yes. Was. Let's keep that in the past tense."

There's a knock at the door a few minutes later. Vin goes to answer it while I bring out the sandwiches and finger food I bought for today. Hosting isn't really my thing but for practical reasons I couldn't exactly do this at someone else's place. We've got food. We've got music. I think I'm doing okay.

Mya enters the kitchen holding a case of beer. She gives me a quick hug.

"It's still so weird to see you with a boyfriend," she says.

I grin. "I know, right? I have a man. I'm hosting parties. I made punch. *Who is she?*"

Casey comes in next with Andre right behind her. She puts a covered plate of cookies on the kitchen counter.

"Thanks for inviting us!"

Everyone is here. I guess it's time to get this party started.

"Listen up, everybody!"

All eyes turn to me.

"The reason we invited you all here this afternoon isn't just for a party. It's because I had something I wanted to tell you."

Sensing the change in tone, Mya leans over and turns the music off. Milo sits down on the couch next to her and grabs her hand. Casey crosses her arms over her middle protectively before moving closer to Andre.

"Um, seven years ago my life changed for the first time. Then five years ago it changed again. But that's the past and I'm looking forward to the future."

I glance over at Vin, who nods encouragingly.

"Anyway, that's why you're here. To help me celebrate something that's really important to me."

I reach up for the ribbon I attached to the ceiling earlier. With one yank, a massive banner unrolls. It spells out the words CANCER FREE in huge pink letters.

I take a little breath and then start doing the dance I practiced. Then I sing at the top of my lungs.

Check One. Check Two.

I want to share some news with you!

Hip thrust.

My humps. My bumps.

Now my ta-tas have no lumps!

Booty shake.

I end with my arms over my head. I look over at Vin who is shaking his head in disbelief.

Since no one is reacting appropriately to my awesome news I figure maybe they need to hear it again.

Check One. Check Two.

Mya jumps up. "Wait a minute. Just hold on."

I let my arms fall back to my sides. "I guess you guys might have some questions."

"*Ariana,*" she whispers tearfully.

Oh crap. This is what I knew would happen. If she cries then I'll cry and I promised myself that nobody was frickin' crying at my party. This is supposed to be a cele-bration.

Casey comes closer and threads her arm through mine. The guys back off, tactfully giving us some space.

"I'm sorry, okay? I just didn't know how to tell you that my boobs tried to kill me. It's not the easiest conversation starter."

Mya puts a shaky hand to her chest. "You said seven years ago?"

"And five years ago. It came back," I remind her softly.

Suddenly she gasps. "That time you had to go out of town. When you said you were getting a boob job—"

"It *was* a boob job. Technically. Just not the kind you thought. I had a tumor removed. And some radiation."

With every word Mya's face falls further. Then she hurtles herself into my arms. I hug her back, overwhelmed with how lucky I am to have friends who love me this much.

Casey wipes her eyes. "I'm so glad you're okay."

I give her a hug, too.

The guys are watching with that awkward energy men always have when they don't want to get emotional. To be honest, all the estrogen in the room is making me a little lightheaded too so I decide it's time for cake.

Vin comes over and kisses my forehead. "You okay, baby?"

I nod. It's time to clear some of the depressing vibes from this room.

"Okay, I can't handle all this sappiness. Come on, guys. It's time to eat my *I beat cancer* cake!"

I retrieve it from the refrigerator and unwrap it. Then I place it in the center of the card table I set up just for this purpose. They all gather round.

Andre sees it first and clamps his lips together, trying not to laugh. When Casey stands on tiptoe to see what he's looking at, her mouth falls open.

The cake I got at the bakery the prior day has been wrapped in brown paper while it was in the refrigerator. I didn't want to scandalize anyone on the street while I was walking to my car. Also, I figured Vin deserved to be surprised just like everyone else.

It's shaped like two huge boobs. The nipples are made with little red candies. It says *Suck It Cancer!* in pink icing.

Mya gasps. "Ari!"

I shrug. "It's my party and I'll have ta-ta cake if I want to!"

Once we've cut pieces and handed them out, the mood in the room lifts considerably. Someone turns the music back on and before long Casey and Andre are dancing like they think they're alone.

Those two still have big honeymoon energy.

Mya and I are talking in the kitchen when Vin comes in. He's looking at me in that way that promises dirty things later.

She elbows me. "I know that look. I'm getting out of the line of fire." She goes to join her husband on the couch.

And then I'm in Vin's arms.

My favorite place to be.

He kisses the top of my head. "When I told you to be sensitive, I must admit I wasn't expecting a song and dance."

"You know me. Never a dull moment."

His eyes shine. "This may be a bit insensitive but how soon can we kick them out? I want to be alone with you."

I splutter with laughter. "We invited them here!"

Then he licks his lips and all I can think of is that deliciously dirty mouth. It's an actual ache that sets up camp right between my thighs.

"Vin? You have to stop looking at me like that," I whisper.

But as usual, my man knows what I really need.

And delivers.

"Everybody get out!" Vin shouts, before walking to the front door and holding it open.

The music turns off abruptly as the others scramble to grab their things, looking around in confusion.

"Nice party," Andre comments before Vin shoves him out the door.

"Get your shit and leave. My girl needs me to rock her world."

I can still hear their laughter echoing down the hallway once he slams the door behind them.

"You are so damn crazy. But I love it." I kiss his face, still laughing.

"I love you, too." Vin leans his forehead against mine. "Ari, the things I feel for you, they're so big. I can't keep them inside."

"You don't have to keep anything locked up anymore. I love you."

He takes my hand. "I know you don't like to move too fast. And I know you hate all that fake romantic shit, anyway. So I'm not asking you to marry me."

I gasp when he pulls a ring from his pocket.

His eyes hold mine. "You don't have to call it an engagement ring. Just as long as you promise to love me, live with me, and cause trouble with me for the rest of our lives."

I sniffle as I squeeze his hand. "The rest of our lives, huh? That's a really long time."

His eyes search mine worriedly.

"Don't panic. This is me *not* asking you to marry me, remember?"

I leap into his arms, knowing he'll always catch me. Then I whisper-yell against his lips.

"This is me *not* saying yes."

I hope you enjoyed *Need Me*!

Anya's book, *Want Me,* is available now. Her story crosses timelines with this book so you'll get to see the other side of the Ariana-Anya pact!

Keep reading for an excerpt of Andre's book, ASK ME! Although I have to warn you, this book is best avoided if you are in any danger of peeing when you laugh. You'll understand when you get to the unicorn scene. Just... trust me.

Author's Note

Want a free book? (and really, who doesn't?)

Become one of Minx's Minions! I reward my evil followers well :) Join at mmalonebooks.com

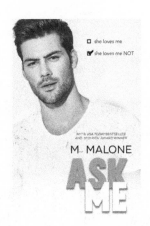

DING DONG I JUST GOT DITCHED

Andre

I'm *that* guy. The one women want and other men want *to be*.

Arrogant? Maybe.

Accurate? Abso-F'ing-lutely.

So when my brother dares me to hit on women as a regular guy, I'm up for the challenge. It turns out quite a few ladies like ripped jeans just as much as haute couture. Except for one. Casey. Nothing I do impresses this girl which only makes me want her more. For the first time, I'm smitten.

Until she ditches me after a night of intense passion.

Casey

If it's possible to screw up a good thing, I'm the girl who'll figure out how. So when I get a new job, I celebrate with one last night of fun before focusing on climbing the corporate ladder.

Until my night of fun walks into the office and I discover who he really is. My firm's biggest client and my new nightmare.

Egotistical, entitled and infuriating, Andre Lavin is not making it easy for me to ignore him. In a battle of wills, we'll see who can hold out the longest.

And who is still standing at the end.

ASK ME is the kind of outrageous romantic comedy that will have you clutching your pearls and laughing until you cry! This standalone romance features crossover characters from the USA TODAY bestselling book BEG ME.

Get ASK ME Now

at minxmalone.com/askme

Excerpt of *ASK ME*

© October 2018 M. Malone

ANDRE

I push through the revolving door and into the lobby of the Madison building. Jason is already in the waiting area talking on his phone. Philippe should have been here already, too. I glance at my watch and then scowl at the time.

This is our third meeting with our marketing agency in the last month and I have no confidence this one will go any better than the last two.

Not that I can voice that opinion. Apparently I've been difficult to work with lately so anything I say will be taken negatively.

Kate rushes into the lobby looking harried. "Mr. Lavin! You're here early." She gives Jason a hard look before pulling out her phone.

I don't respond, unsure why being early requires a warning.

Jason shrugs. "I was trying to call you. Our last meeting ended early. Hopefully James can accommodate us."

"Of course! I'm sure it's fine." Her voice is upbeat but her fingers fly over the screen of her phone frantically.

Who could she be texting right now when we have a meeting to attend?

Jason leans over. "She's probably warning everyone upstairs that the dragon has left his lair." He chuckles when Kate glares at him.

I hit the button for the elevator. The past month has been a test of my patience in every way. Although I originally planned to stay in the States during this brand transition, last week I made the decision to go back to Milan for the duration. Why stay in a concrete prison enduring rain and questionable air quality when I could be at home, enjoying the exceptional weather and exquisite food?

"I'm ready to get this meeting done. We have a schedule to keep," I grumble, already irritated. We're flying back to Italy in just a few hours and another pointless meeting is not how I want to spend my time before getting on a plane.

Jason clears his throat before glancing at me. "So, before we attend this meeting maybe we should nail down what we hope to accomplish today. The last couple of meetings have been a little chaotic."

"Meaning that I've hated everything they've come up with." I adjust my tie slightly in the mirror image on the elevator doors.

He shifts next to me. "Meaning that you've made up your mind to hate everything because you've been in a shitty mood for what feels like six months straight."

My hand pauses on my tie.

After Jason broke the news that the investigators couldn't find Casey, I thought I'd come to terms with it. But even after I called off the official investigation, she was never far from my thoughts. I couldn't stop thinking about her at the most random moments and my lack of focus did not go unnoticed.

So I threw myself into my work with a vengeance, staying later at the office and coming in earlier. Maybe I was subconsciously punishing myself for allowing the most captivating woman I've ever met to slip through my fingers or maybe I truly thought that work could help me forget. But that time, Philippe was the one given the task of telling me that several of my staff members were on the verge of quitting.

Now I've reached a point where I have to accept that this isn't something I can fix. No amount of hard work or dedication will right this situation.

"You're right. I haven't been myself."

Jason looks stunned at my agreement but just then the elevator doors slide open. The head of the agency is waiting there to greet us, with the two lead marketing executives who have been working on our account standing directly behind him. Mya Taylor and Milo Hamilton worked together on the campaign that launched Lavin Bridal into a very successful year. Approving the campaign for that launch wasn't nearly so difficult and I can concede that it was entirely due to my state of mind.

Clumsy Girl is gone, as surely as if she was just a figment of my imagination. I've heard it from everyone over the last month: Jason, my brother and even the bartender at the bar I can't seem to stay away from.

She's gone.

It sucks the way things ended but I have to accept that it did end. Casey and I had a brief, magical moment and it changed me.

Maybe that's all it was meant to do.

I extend my hand. "James, I apologize for arriving so early. I hope we haven't inconvenienced you too greatly."

He shakes my hand and then motions to the others. "It's no problem at all. The team has put together a fantastic presentation for you today."

As he's speaking, my eyes are drawn to the reception desk behind him. A young woman stands and then when she notices me, freezes. But she's not the one I'm looking at. No, all of my attention is on the young woman sitting behind the desk, her attention fixed on her computer. She's wearing some type of headset and her dark hair is twisted up into a bun. But there's no mistaking that face.

That adorable, frustrating face.

Clumsy Girl is here.

My feet move forward without my permission as I walk away from James, leaving Jason and Kate to continue with the pleasantries. I'm definitely being rude but that's something I'll have to deal with later. After looking for her so long, maybe this is where I finally crack. Hell, the woman I'm staring at is probably a sixty-year-old grandmother and my mind is simply superimposing the image I've longed to see.

Then she looks up and sees me. Her face freezes into a mask of horror. After a few seconds where we stare at each other in mutual disbelief, she murmurs something to the woman next to her.

And that's when I get angry.

"James, please introduce me to your new receptionist. I don't think I've had the pleasure."

Everyone stills at my command. Or maybe because my voice feels abnormally loud. I clear my throat and smooth my tie, mainly to keep my hands busy so they don't reach out and grab the woman staring back at me defiantly from behind the desk.

"Of course. Mr. Lavin, this is Cassandra Michaels. She's been here with us for about two months and has been a great asset to the team."

While he talks I hold Casey's gaze, delighted by how her cheeks flush red under the praise. She darts a glance over at me and then does an awkward half wave, as if I'll settle for that. But I've spent the last two months searching for her after she gave me a fake name so I'm not letting her off that easily.

I approach the reception desk with my hand outstretched, knowing that she'll have to get up and shake it or appear rude.

She swallows, the sound audible. But she stands and walks around the desk. Or at least, she tries to. However, it appears she's forgotten that her headset is connected to the computer so as she walks away, the cord yanks her back and she lands sprawled on the floor.

Staring right up between my legs.

"Kill me now."

Her voice was barely above a whisper but everyone else must have heard it too because I hear choking sounds behind me that can only be laughter.

"Are you okay, Casey?" James appears at my elbow with a hand outstretched to help her up. But there's no way he's touching her before I do. So I lean down and extend a hand. She looks hesitant but finally takes it.

"I'm so sorry, sir."

Hearing her call me that takes me from shock to outrage. Sir? Like I'm some stranger she's meeting for the first time? I have a sudden overwhelming urge to remind her just how well we know each other but the pleading look in her eyes stops me.

"Please. Don't get me fired," she whispers, turning her head away slightly so James can't hear.

"There is nothing to be sorry for," I say loud enough for everyone to hear.

Then I bring her hand to my mouth and dust a kiss over her knuckles. The gesture will look polite to anyone watching but Casey sucks in a sudden breath.

James and the others have already started talking amongst themselves about the meeting. No one is paying attention to us right now. They don't feel the heat being generated right at their feet.

"I can't say the sight of you in any position is something to apologize for," I finish in a voice for her alone.

When she sees that no one is looking anymore, Casey rips her hand from mine. "What are you doing here?"

"I have a meeting," I reply, knowing the casual response will annoy her. But who can blame me for wanting to see those honey eyes light up with fire again? I've seen just how passionate she can get, after all.

She pulls off her headset with a frustrated huff. "Look, what happened between us ... We should just forget about it. Right? We can do that."

"What am I supposed to forget exactly? How much fun we had talking in the bar that night? Or that we spent hours bringing each other pleasure? That I've never felt anything like that with another woman? Which part is supposed to be so forgettable?"

My bold statement is met with a glare before she plasters on a wide smile. "Of course, Mr. Lavin. It was so nice to meet you, too!"

When I turn, I catch Jason's eye. He's staring at Casey but I don't think he's recognized her yet.

The others have started walking toward the hallway that leads to the conference room. I can't stay here too much longer without drawing undue attention which is exactly what Casey has asked me not to do.

Her eyes turn pleading. *"Please, don't make a scene.* I need this job."

As angry as I am, I can't ignore the desperation in her voice. She told me that night at the bar she was celebrating getting a new job, one she was very excited and grateful for. No matter how pissed I was to wake up alone, I wouldn't want to take that from her.

"I won't say anything."

Her shoulders drop in relief and she lets out a sigh that reminds me a little too much of the sounds she made that night in my arms. It definitely pricks at my ego that she seems to have no problem moving on from the night we shared when I've been haunted by it ever since. Could it be possible that the night that was life changing for me was only average for her?

Then our eyes meet again and she shivers. Heat explodes between us and I have to clench my hands into fists to keep from reaching out for her. No, she feels this, too. But wants to deny it for some reason.

"Thank you. For not saying anything. You should go. Everyone is staring."

"I'll go. But Casey," I wait until she meets my eyes. "I won't be forgetting about that night anytime soon. And neither will you."

Get ASK ME Now
at minxmalone.com/askme

BEG ME (Milo & Mya)

My rooster is on strike. Yeah, I can't believe it either. But he'll only crow for one woman. Spoiler Alert *she hates me*

ASK ME (Andre & Casey)

Am I arrogant? Maybe. Do women still want me? Abso-F'ing-lutely. Then I meet the one woman who isn't impressed.

NEED ME (Vin & Ariana)

Crazy sh*t every day keeps relationships away. Except there's one guy who just *keeps* showing up. And if I'm not careful, I might get used to needing someone.

WANT ME (Law & Anya)

No strings attached. Sounds good, right? Except if I'm not her boyfriend ... the position is open for someone else.

* Join my VIP list for FREE books *

newsletter.mmalonebooks.com

Just One Thing : Scientist Bennett Alexander is a bona fide genius but he still can't figure out how to "get the girl". So he hires a dating tutor. What could go wrong? Other than falling for his teacher, of course.

Bad King: My parents just put a gold diggers target on my back. But if all they want is a wedding, I can do that. I'll find the fiancee of their nightmares. *Who Wants to Marry a Billionaire? Must be completely inappropriate.*

Bad Blood : I'd do anything for my best friend's little sister. Until she asks for the one thing I can't give. One night. No rules. *2019 RITA® Award Winner!*

Blue-Collar Billionaires

Billions from the deadbeat dad they never knew sounds pretty sweet. Until they find out what he really wants.

Tank / Finn / Gabe / Zack / Luke

- ROMANTIC SUSPENSE -

(Co-authored with Nana Malone)

- The Shameless Trilogy
- The Force Duet
- The Deep Duet
- The Sin Duet

- The Brazen Duet

- PARANORMAL ROMANCE -

Nathan's Heart

The Brotherhood of Bandits

ABOUT THE AUTHOR

M. Malone is a RITA® Award winner and a NYT & USA Today Bestselling author of completely inappropriate romantic comedy. She spends most days wearing Wonder Woman leggings and T-shirts that she's embarrassed for anyone to see while she plays with her imaginary friends.

She lives with her husband and their two sons in the picturesque mountains of Northern Virginia even though she is afraid of insects, birds, butterflies and other humans.

She also holds a Master's degree in Business from a prestigious college that would no doubt be scandalized at how she's using her expensive education.

facebook.com/minxmalone

twitter.com/minxmalone

instagram.com/minxmalone

bookbub.com/authors/m-malone